THE
HODGKISS
MYSTERIES

Curtains for Hodgkiss

Hodgkiss and the Miraculous Message

Hodgkiss and the Erroneous email

PETER SINCLAIR

About the author

Peter Sinclair has spent most of his working life writing. He began reporting courts and councils in rural Orange (NSW) in the late 1950s then worked briefly for *The Sydney Daily Telegraph* where, because of his fluent shorthand, he was sentenced first to report local councils then banished to the Coroner's Court.

He'd had enough of sudden death and murder when opportunity knocked and he joined the staff of a new, large weekly paper in Sydney's northern suburbs, *The North Shore Times* where he was soon reporting councils again.

In 1965, he climbed over the journalistic fence to work as press secretary for a succession of NSW cabinet ministers (both Liberal and Labor) until 1991. Since then, he has made guest reappearances to help out in the PR sections of government departments.

His absorbing hobby is playing the piano. He has made a number of CDs in very limited editions. The titles tell it all: Peter Murders Mozart, Wrecks Rachmaninoff and Desecrates Debussy. He says he gives them away to people he doesn't like!

He has been married to Margaret for fifty-seven years and they have two sons; Sam, who is married to Carolyn with one son, Harry, 18, and Patrick who is married to Beejai with twin boys, Jackson and Zachary, aged 13.

Published in Australia by Peter Sinclair

First published in Australia 2020
Copyright © Peter Sinclair 2020
Cover design, typesetting: Chameleon Print Design

The right of Peter Sinclair to be identified as the Author of the Work has been asserted in accordance with the Copyright, Designs and Patents Act 1988.

The Hodgkiss Mysteries Volume X
ISBN: 978-0-6489252-7-9
Sinclair, Peter
pp196

For Margaret

Author's Note

I t has been no easy task to assemble material in order to reconstruct these accounts of the extraordinary contributions which Edgar Hodgkiss made to criminal detection over the years in which he was active in the field.

Hodgkiss himself kept no records.

When he suggested solutions to investigations being undertaken by his son-in-law, Detective Sergeant Donald Burke, Hodgkiss was convinced that he was merely stating the obvious and that his contributions were unremarkable and not worthy of record.

However, this presumption that he was 'merely stating the obvious' was frequently the cause of acrimony between himself and Sergeant Burke who resented the implied slur on his own powers of observation.

Fortunately for readers of these reports (and for posterity), Hodgkiss's daughter, Esme, kept detailed records in a series of exercise books which she has kindly made available to those of us interested in researching and recording the contributions made by this unique character.

Jan Campbell-Jones, the General Manager of Kanundda Council during this testing period of its history, also kindly consented to assist by releasing relevant documents from her personal files and from council's own official records system.

Ms Campbell-Jones also graciously agreed to be interviewed and has given accounts of many of these extraordinary events from her point of view, relying on her remarkable powers of recall to provide in some cases verbatim accounts of significant conversations. In addition she has allowed us access to the many emails that passed between Hodgkiss and herself. Hodgkiss, of course, had deleted these emails from his laptop within days, or in some instances, within hours of transmission.

I am indebted also to the many members of community organisations who supported Edgar Hodgkiss in his various campaigns against what he saw as the deficiencies of Kanundda Council and who have helped me verify many important details.

Readers of these records should note that they do not appear in chronological order therefore minor temporal inconsistencies may appear.

Many incidents in which Hodgkiss played an important role have not yet been committed to paper and many others, unfortunately, will never appear on the public record.

On occasions both the innocent and the guilty must be protected.

Peter Sinclair,
Lillimoor, 2011

Curtains for Hodgkiss

'Esme, you can not be serious.'

Edgar Hodgkiss slammed down the heavy typescript on the round redwood table.

He added: 'This is the most appalling piece of pap I have ever had the misfortune to read.'

Across the table his daughter, Esme Burke, looked both embarrassed and defensive.

But Hodgkiss wasn't finished. 'Who wrote this stuff anyway? Have you any idea?'

'Fellow by the name of Roberts. It's there on the front page.'

'Yes, I can read, thank you, Esme. But who is he? Who is this ...' he glanced down at the script ... 'Chester Roberts? Have you any idea?'

'Not really. I've only met him once at the casting session. Besides, what's wrong with it may I ask? I don't remember *you* ever writing a play.'

Hodgkiss frowned. 'Really, Esme. That's hardly the point. And I can assure you that if I ever decided to apply myself to writing a play it would be infinitely better than this bit of appalling rubbish. Even Donald objects to it and he's no great judge of the written word.'

Esme shook her head vigourously. 'That's not true, Dad. Donald didn't say he objects to the play. All he said was …'

'That I object to you being in it.'

Detective Inspector Donald Burke stepped out onto the back deck of the Burke's family home in suburban Lillimoor to join his wife and father-in-law.

'And I've got every good reason to object,' Donald continued angrily. 'I don't want my wife prancing around on stage half naked in front of a couple of hundred strangers.'

'Donald, that's ridiculous. I'm playing the part of a French maid and everyone knows what they always wear … a skirt and a little frilly apron. It's really just a kind of uniform.'

'Yeah! Little apron's right. Next to nothing. That's what they wear. Some uniform! Well, I think it's a disgrace. Really, Esme, I don't know what got into you volunteering to do it. To tell you the truth I thought you'd have more sense.'

Before Esme could reply Hodgkiss cut in. 'The part of the French maid is typical of what's wrong with the play. The whole thing's jam-packed with all of the oldest, corniest, most dated clichés imaginable: mistaken identity, twins, scorned lovers, bumbling detectives, French maids … the lot.'

Donald took up the theme: 'Not to mention a murder scene where the victim's tied to a chair with a knife stuck in his chest. Utter corn.'

Hodgkiss nodded agreement. 'Yes, and that's followed immediately by a black out on stage and a quick curtain for dramatic effect. I don't know how many times I've seen something like that in third rate amateur dramatic productions.'

'Well I think the audience will love it,' said Esme.

Hodgkiss feigned surprise. 'Do you mean that you seriously expect people to pay good money to turn up to witness this bit of nonsense?' he asked sceptically.

'Well, for your information, Dad, we've got lots of advance bookings already. So there.'

'Then all I can say is that a fool and his money are soon parted.'

Esme glanced at them both uneasily. 'Well I might as well tell the two of you now: you'd better get to like it because you're both going to be in it.'

Donald and Hodgkiss looked at her open-mouthed.

Esme continued defiantly. 'Yes, I've volunteered both of you so you had better get used to the idea.'

'Well you can just un-volunteer me,' said Donald. 'No way known will I be in a play, especially one like this. And what do you expect me to do, ponce around on stage dressed as a butler or something silly like that?'

'No, of course not, Donald. I wouldn't do that to you or to Dad. I didn't put you down for a part in the play. Besides I don't think either of you would be up to doing it.'

'Oh really. Well when I was at school ...'

'I've put you down for prompt, Donald.'

'Prompt!? Whatever is prompt?'

'You just tell the actors their lines when they forget them.'

Hodgkiss muttered. 'Then I expect Donald will be very busy indeed.'

'But how on earth am I going to tell them their lines?' Donald demanded. 'I've never even read the stupid play.'

Esme shook her head impatiently. 'Don't be silly, Donald. No one expects you to learn the whole thing off by heart. You've just got to sit in the prompt box with a copy of the script and if any of the actors forget their lines you prompt them. It happens with all plays. Even the big-time professional productions. They all have a prompter.'

'And where will I be sitting? In the front row?'

'Of course not. There's a special little cubby hole near the front of the stage and just to one side … somewhere the audience can't see you. You'll just sit in there and follow the play on your script. Right?'

'And what vital function have you volunteered me for?' Hodgkiss asked.

'You'll do the curtains and be the stage hand. That means you'll have to pull the ropes to open and close the curtains at the right time and make sure that everything on the stage, like tables and chairs and things, are where they should be at the start of every scene. It's a very responsible job, Dad, so I don't want you to make a fuss about it.'

'Who said anything about making a fuss?' Secretly Hodgkiss was pleased at the prospect of being involved.

'Well, that's a first,' said Esme. 'I thought you'd scream the house down.'

'Really, Esme,' said Hodgkiss, 'I don't think I have ever done anything to stand in the way of your ambitions.'

'Ambitions!' Esme exclaimed. 'Oh come one, Dad, you don't think for one moment that I've got serious ambitions to be an actress? This is just a bit of fun and a chance to raise some money for charity. That's all it is.'

'Well I am delighted to hear that.'

'I'm not under any illusions about the whole thing. I know it's just an amateur production. For heavens' sake, they're even using a bicycle bell for a telephone ringing.'

Hodgkiss nodded. 'I suppose that says it all, doesn't it.'

'But that doesn't mean that we shouldn't all take our parts seriously,' Esme cautioned. She turned to her husband. 'Now,

Donald, I want you to read that script carefully from start to finish.'

Donald began to protest. 'But I thought you said ...'

'I said you don't have to learn it all off by heart, but you *do* have to make yourself very familiar with it ... every word, so that you can give any of the actors their lines if they seem to have forgotten them. It's not rocket science, Donald. You've only got to be able to read.'

She turned to her father. 'And you, Dad. Later in the week I will give you diagrams of where exactly each piece of furniture and each other item, like rugs and decanters and things, have to be placed in each scene of the play and it's your job to make sure that everything is in place before you pull the curtain for that scene. Is that clear? Not a terribly difficult job if you ask me.'

Hodgkiss nodded. 'I understand the role of the stage hand in a production thank you Esme. I do not expect to find it too demanding.'

Esme stood. 'Good then that's settled.'

Donald and Hodgkiss looked at each other but said nothing.

*　　*　　*

'Mate, it's brilliant. You're a genius.'

Mayor of Kanundda, Kevin Feather, was unstinting in his praise. He continued. 'Best play ever. It's got everything: murder, mystery and of course sex.'

'The French maid, you mean,' suggested the proud author, Chester Roberts.

'Yeah, it was a stroke of genius putting her in. Who've you found for the part? Got to have a good little body, eh?'

Roberts consulted a list of names in a folder in front of him. 'Esme Burke's her name.'

'What's she like?' the mayor inquired. 'Hot?'

'Maybe sort of hot. She's not young exactly. About mid to late thirties I'd say at a guess. Maybe forty.'

Mayor Feather sniggered. 'Well there's many a good tune been played on an old violin, eh?'

'Well I wouldn't get my hopes up too far in that direction, Kevin. Her old man'll be on deck for most of the time she's there and he's a copper. He's doing prompt.'

'Doing prompt? What the hell d'you mean by that… doing prompt.'

'The person doing prompt feeds the actors their lines when … if they forget them,' Roberts explained.

'Well it's not going to be much of a show if you've got a lot of actors who can't even remember their lines.'

Cr Barry McCann, sitting opposite the mayor, explained: 'It's just an amateur production, mate. None of these people are getting paid.'

'Then it's not going to be much of a show is it? So why are we putting up the money to put it on if they're just a bunch of amateurs? There won't be much in it for us, will there?'

'Just the kudos, mate,' McCann explained.

'Kudos?' the mayor queried.

'You know: brownie points. We want brownie points for being patrons of the arts. Remember the old theatre project we're working on.'

Mayor Feather nodded, light dawning. 'Right. Now I've gotcha. Brownie points. Yeah.' He smiled.

McCann continued. 'And if all the punters out there realise that we're such patrons of the arts then it'll be so much easier to put the deal across with the old theatre building. Right?'

'Yeah, right.' He frowned. 'But we're not really going to put on plays in that old dump, are we?'

'No, of course we're not,' said McCann impatiently. 'But that's the story we've got to run to get our hands on the place.'

Mayor Feather nodded, smiling happily. 'Then once we've got it we do it up then put in units and shops. Right?'

'Yeah. That's the plan, but don't forget the cinema. We've got to put a little cinema in or some people'll scream blue murder because we promised to keep the place as a centre for the arts.'

'Yeah, right. A cinema.'

'A *boutique* cinema,' McCann corrected. 'Fifty seats I think it says in the plan.'

'That's very boutique,' said Roberts.

'You can't get any boutique-er and that's the way we want it.'

Mayor Feather asked: 'Is there any way we could put on this play at the new theatre … as an official opening or something like that. It's a great play you've written here Chester. It's got absolutely everything going for it. I especially love the bit where the guy's tied up to the chair and gets murdered with a knife in his chest. Say, how do you think of things like that, and how do you manage that bit with the knife; make it look as if the guy's been stabbed. I mean it'd have to be done properly or the whole thing'd look corny.'

'Don't worry about that, Kevin,' Roberts said. 'It's all taken care of. The knife's only plastic and it'll have a retractable blade and it's made so it'll stick to the man's chest after he's stabbed. It'll look real enough, don't worry about that. It's all taken care of. Wonderful place, the theatre.'

He added: 'Trouble with putting the play on in the new place is that the cinema won't have a proper stage for a play or dressing rooms or nearly enough seats to make it worth-while putting it on. Besides, I wouldn't get ahead of myself with making plans. We're not there yet. There's still one or two problems in the way.'

'Bloody Archer, d'you mean?'

'Yeah, bloody Archer.'

'Yeah … and the bloody fire regulations.'

Roberts frowned. 'But I thought you'd got that sorted. I thought you had a mate in the fire brigades who was going to do the right thing.'

McCann nodded. 'Yeah, well he hasn't got back to me yet.'

'Well nothing's going to happen 'til we've got approval from that lot. We won't be able to have workmen set foot in the building until it meets every last one of the fire regulations.'

'Tell me something I don't know,' McCann snapped. 'Look, I've got it sorted, right, so don't go on about it.'

'Mate, it'd better be sorted or we're nowhere, right?'

Mayor Feather wriggled out of his swivel chair and headed for the large blonde wood art deco bar behind against the side wall.

'Well, who's for a free drink?' he asked. 'Scotch and ice everyone? Here, I'll get Fred in to fix the drinks for us.'

He walked across to the door, pulled it open and put his head out. 'Fred. Got a moment?'

A short, middle-aged man wearing on his face an habitual discontented scowl wandered into the room.

'Pour us a few drinks would you, Fred. Scotch and ice all round, and have one yourself.' Then a thought occurred to him. 'Fred, how'd you like to be in our new play?'

Fred turned from the bar. 'I don't know about that, Mr Mayor. I ain't never been in no plays. Not much good at remembering lines.'

'Well, we could get you a part without too many lines.'

Fred shook his head dubiously. Then he brightened. 'Is there a part for an electrician? I could always do that.'

Mayor Feather chuckled. 'I doubt if there's a part for an electrician but I reckon you could probably do the lighting for the show; you know turning the spotlights on and off at the right time. Things like that. I'll have a talk to my friend Monica Bray and fix it with her. Now, how're those drinks going, Fred? And don't go too far, mate, I want to have a quiet talk to you about something when we're finished here, right.'

Fred turned to the mayor. He smiled an unpleasant gap-toothed grimace. 'I'll be just outside the door, boss.'

*   *   *

Monica Bray stood in the middle of the stage and looked about at the cast and crew standing in a semi-circle around her, mouths open, eyes expectant.

How often in her career, such as it was, had she stood in some old, inadequate school hall confronting almost identical groups of bumbling stage hands and men and women whose ambitions far exceeded their talents.

She sighed then tried to smile although she understood already that the production was a disaster in the making.

The two principals hated the sight of each other and for the very best of all possible reasons; the leading lady, Victoria Anderson, was until very recently the mistress of the leading man, Ronald Archer, who had dumped her in the most humiliating and public way.

Even now Vicki was looking daggers at Ronnie who was ostentatiously looking at the French maid with more than passing interest.

And that sleazy type someone had cast for the police inspector was already feeling the housemaid's bottom and she wasn't protesting.

Monica saw storm warnings everywhere she looked.

And that French maid; for heaven's sake, talk about mutton dressed up as lamb. Still she looked vaguely intelligent and did not seem to have an attitude problem like one or two of the other minor players who no doubt would be displaying temperament before the day was much older.

Esme Burke, yes that was her name, was a distinct improvement on the two other girls who had read for the role of the French maid. She was perhaps a little older and plumper but the other two both had heads on them like the proverbial robber's dog, so choosing Esme had been a no-brainer.

And as for the crew; one superannuee to pull the curtains and see to the properties; well, at least he looked intelligent. And the other fellow, David or was it Douglas Burke, the old chap's son-in-law — a copper someone had told her — was going to do the prompting. I just hope he's an improvement on the fellow I had in my last production. He couldn't read without moving his lips, grunting and sliding his finger along the lines. Then he slept through most of the show anyway and the actors were left to ad lib when they forgot their lines, which was frequently.

Today Mr what's-his-name, the copper, Burke — that was it — would have to do sound effects because she hadn't managed to find someone for that task. Besides, prompting would not be needed at this stage.

She clapped her hands together. 'What fun we shall have!' she exclaimed, smiling ferociously.

Then she slipped into serious down-to-business mode. 'Now I know you are all familiar with your parts although you won't be word perfect just yet. That will come, and if you do happen to have a problem remembering a line we will have …' here she paused to consult her thick ring-bind folder to find the right Christian name … 'we have Mr Donald Burke to help you out.' She turned towards Donald and smiled broadly.

'Thank you, Donald. I'm sure we'll appreciate your help from time to time during rehearsals although I'm quite confident that you won't be overworked during our actual performances.' Like hell he won't, she thought. If it's anything like the last show he'll probably have to say more lines than the leads.

She continued: 'But for the present, while we are still reading our parts, Donald will be doing sound effects for us.'

Eyes swiveled towards Donald who smiled awkwardly and nodded.

Ms Bray continued. 'Before we start our first read-through I want to congratulate Mr …' another quick glance at the folder … 'Mr Chester Roberts for presenting us with such a wonderful script.

'He has a fine ear for dialogue and a great feeling for the dramatic moment and how to get it across.'

A female voice, not identifiable muttered: 'Every vacuous cliché in the history of the theatre.'

The police inspector raised a hand.

Again Ms Bray stole a quick look at her folder. 'Yes, Mr … um … Jefferson?'

'Shouldn't the police inspector have a sergeant to help with the investigation? On all the police programmes on television the inspector always …'

Ms Bray's patience was beginning to ebb already. 'Yes, I'm sure that's the case on TV but unfortunately we don't have the same sort of budget those shows have to play around with.'

But Mr Jefferson was not satisfied. 'Well, I don't see how I can be expected to solve a murder without a sergeant to do all the leg work. You ask Mr Burke there … he's a real-life policeman.'

But before Donald could be drawn into the crossfire Ms Bray saved the day. 'I'm afraid we mere mortals must accept the script as it is presented to us by the author. That's the way the theatre works.' She pressed on quickly. 'Now, before we begin our read-through do any of you have any more questions?'

Victoria Anderson raised a hand.

'Yes, Victoria,' Ms Bray asked, now feeling faintly bilious. 'What is it?'

'I was wondering where the dressing rooms for the stars are located?' the female lead inquired, eyes wide.

Ms Bray attempted a look of baffled innocence. 'But we've already seen the dressing room, Vicki. We left our coats and things there.'

Victoria Anderson's eyes flew wider. 'Dressing room! Did you say that was our dressing room? You don't call that cupboard a dressing room, surely? Are you telling me that there are no separate arrangements for the female lead?'

Now Ms Bray attempted a conciliatory smile. 'I'm afraid we are only a small company, Victoria, and we must take what is given us.'

'Do you mean to say that we must all change in the one space? That is quite intolerable.'

'You may have noticed that there is a number of tall, sturdy screens that will allow us to divide the boys from the girls and give all members of the cast adequate privacy for the very few changes that must be made. And I assume that we all have suitable mirrors at home that we can bring along for our make-up.'

'It's a sort of do-it-yourself show, then,' muttered the police inspector.

Ms Bray clapped her hands again, this time with less enthusiasm. 'Now, we all have our scripts with us, do we?'

It turned out that the inspector had left his at home so the chambermaid volunteered to share hers with him, a kindly gesture that was rewarded with another pinch of her bottom.

'So, I think we'll just have a quick read-through to start with, just to get a feel for the play. Act one, scene one. I think that calls for the housemaid and the two principals. The rest of you can take a short break. Now, Mr Burke, if you wouldn't mind doing the sound effects for this scene. I don't think the script makes very heavy demands at this point.'

Donald looked about. 'Where is it ... the sound effects gear?'

Ms Bray waved a vague hand towards the offstage. 'The equipment should be over there. I left it on a small wooden table in the wings somewhere. It's all there ... everything you'll need.'

Donald retreated into the wings to find a folding card table littered with an assortment of odd items.

Ms Bray called. 'Now let's get this show on the road. A doorbell, if you please, Mr Burke.'

Donald hunted furiously among the assorted items for something likely to simulate the sound of a doorbell. The only item likely to meet the requirement was a bicycle bell.

He rang it.

'That's the telephone, Mr Burke,' Ms Bray called, her patience obviously fraying.

Donald looked about desperately. 'There's no other bell here that I can see, Ms Bray,' he called.

Ms Bray strode angrily across the stage into the wings,

brushed Donald to one side and began to sort through the items on the table. 'Damned things gone,' she snorted. 'Use that instead,' she said pointing to a wooden mallet. 'Well, have a door knocker instead of a bell … right?'

Donald nodded, picking up the hammer and tapping it experimentally against a thick piece of wood nailed to the wall nearby.

'That's the style, Donald. Now, on with the show,' she trilled hurrying back towards the stage.

Seeing that his services obviously were not to be required opening and closing the curtain, Hodgkiss went exploring towards the rear of the old building.

Against the back wall Hodgkiss discovered an antiquated electrical switchboard. He frowned: Now, I wonder who's doing the lighting for this production, he thought, raising a hand to his short, well-trimmed grey beard. Running a dubious eye over the ancient equipment Hodgkiss was thankful that he would not be expected to touch any of the rusting switches.

Whoever it is I hope they have their insurance paid up, he thought.

While he explored the dark corners in the rear of the old building Hodgkiss could hear the bickering on stage.

Victoria was complaining. 'He's chopping off the end of all my lines. Every time. He's doing it deliberately.'

Then Ronald Archer's voice, mocking: 'Darling, I realise that you have to grapple with any words of more than one syllable, but that's no excuse why I should have to delay my delivery. I have taken the trouble to …'

Ms Bray cut him off. 'Perhaps we can just start again from where the housemaid comes in. Thank you Rhonda.'

And so the read-through ground on. Eventually Hodgkiss found himself beside Donald at the sound effects table.

'Have you found the front door yet?' he inquired.

Donald shook his head while concentrating furiously on the text. 'I've got to make the clock strike twelve any minute now. How on earth am I going to do that? There's no clock here.'

'Of course there's no clock here,' said Hodgkiss. 'But there should be a bell or a gong of some sort.' He pointed under the table. 'Try that,' he suggested.

Donald reached down and came up holding in one hand a brass gong suspended in a metal frame and in the other a small padded striker. He set them down on the table and returned anxiously to the text.

'I see it's just gone twelve,' said Victoria in an unnecessarily loud voice.

Donald struck the gone twelve times, quickly.

'How time flies,' Archer commented.

'Stick to the lines, will you, Ronnie,' said Victoria tartly. 'There's no call to comment on the efforts of the stage hands, however incompetent they may be.'

In the wings Donald coloured angrily while Hodgkiss smirked.

Ms Bray ignored this repartee and once again abandoned her post and strode into the wings. 'That gong, Mr Burke, I think is for the dinner sequence in Act Two.'

'Oh, sorry Ms Bray,' said Donald, all confusion, 'but I couldn't see anything else that might have been a clock striking.'

Monica Bray's eye swept over the table, then she stooped to look underneath. 'Someone appears to have taken the clock bell,' she said. 'Never mind. We'll have a look for it later.'

She turned and headed back on-stage where the two leads were now exchanging personal assessments freely and with enthusiasm.

During an interval when hostilities were suspended Hodgkiss found himself standing beside Archer.

'And what do you think of our play, Mr ... er ... Hodgkiss, wasn't it?'

'Edgar Hodgkiss. Yes, well of course I'm not a great judge of the dramatic art, but ...'

'"The dramatic art"', Archer quoted. 'I'm sure our director would be delighted by your description of her appalling effort.'

Hodgkiss continued: ' ... but obviously it is very early days yet and I think the play has a great deal of ... um ... potential, shall we say.'

'Very discreetly put, Mr Hodgkiss. But the whole thing's a stinker ... real amateur hour stuff.'

'Well, I'd find it hard to argue with that, Mr Archer, but let us hope that Ms Bray will manage to tighten things up as everyone settles into their roles. I cannot help but wonder who on earth has put up the money for this awful affair. They're sure to lose every cent.'

Archer turned, surprised. 'Don't you know who's the angel for this essay in disaster? It was council. Council put up the money.'

'Kanundda Council? Are you telling me they've used ratepayers' money to mount this ... shambles?'

'Oh yes. There's no big secret about it. It was all discussed and passed in open council.'

'But I don't remember hearing about it. There was certainly nothing about it in the local paper.'

'Oh no, there wouldn't be. Council didn't want any publicity about it so what did they do? The recommendation for council to finance the show came up for discussion at the end of the agenda when the reporter from the Star was home safely tucked up in bed.'

'But why on earth is council getting involved in something like this?'

'There's a couple reasons for that, Mr Hodgkiss. First one is so that the mayor can give some of his mates something to do to raise their prestige.'

'Mates, which mates are these?' Hodgkiss inquired.

'Well, first of all there's the author of this piece of drivel, Chester Roberts. He's the mayor's cousin. Then there's our director, Monica, another long-term mate. I think she used to help out in his election campaigns. And I wouldn't be surprised to see more of his chums turn up in one capacity or another before much longer.'

'And the second reason?' Hodgkiss inquired.

'The second reason is that council wants to be known far and wide as a patron of the arts. Lot of bloody nonsense of course, because anyone who knows anything about them knows they're a pack of Philistines. Really it's just a scam.'

'A scam? In what way?'

Archer looked hard at Hodgkiss, hesitated, then decided to take the plunge. 'You know that old abandoned theatre in Robson Street?'

Hodgkiss nodded. 'Do you mean the one that had to close when the fellow who owned and operated it was caught embezzling huge sums of money from his own car sales business?'

'That's the chap, fellow by the name of Brass,' said Archer cheerfully. 'Well, after he went to gaol there were no more funds for the theatre and of course it just closed down. Then when he died the theatre itself passed to his son, Edward, and of course now young Edward wants to unload it. But he's got a problem; the fire regulations. You see it's such an old building that the fire board won't let anyone use it for anything because according to them it's a fire trap. One careless match or cigarette butt and the whole thing would go up in flames. There are no proper fire stairs, no emergency lighting, no fire curtains, no alarms ... nothing.'

Hodgkiss nodded agreement. 'Many of those old buildings, and some not so old buildings, are just disasters waiting to happen and neither council nor the fire authorities are prepared to do anything about it for fear of treading on influential toes.'

'Not wrong, Hodgkiss. Disasters waiting to happen ... a good way of putting it.'

'So where does the scam come into it?'

'Well, you see the council, really it's just Mayor Feather and some of his crooked cronies, Barry McCann in particular, reckon they can make a fortune out of the old building if they can only get their hands on it at the right price.'

Hodgkiss shook his head. 'But what would be the use of that. It would never be any use to them for as long as the fire department won't give it a clean bill of health. Until then they can't use if for anything, surely.'

Archer smiled. 'Got it in one, Hodgkiss. That's the point exactly.'

Hodgkiss continued: 'And even if they somehow managed to buy it cheap they'd still have to carry out all the works the fire board insists on before they can do anything with it. And I'm sure they don't think they're going to make much money if they start to operate it as a live theatre again.'

Archer nodded eagerly. 'Of course not. That's the point. They've got no intention of opening it up as a theatre again.' He paused. 'Can you guess what they're planning to do if they get their hands on it?'

'Rezone it, obviously?' Hodgkiss suggested. 'They'd have

to, because they'd never get permission from the government to knock it down because it's a genuine historic building which is more than you can say for the assortment of second rate run-down gerry-built houses they hold up as shining examples of heritage that must be preserved.'

'You're not wrong about that. They'd never be able to knock it down. But they don't have to. They'd only have to change the zoning then, because the building itself is tall and the existing basement so deep, they figure they can put in three floors of home units with parking and shops underneath. And they'd make so much money out of that they could afford to do all the things the fire board says.'

'And might I ask how you happen to know all of this?'

Archer laid a sly finger beside his nose. 'You might ask, Hodgkiss, but I might not tell you. But just you wait and see if I'm right or not.'

'Do you think it's really likely to happen?'

Archer thought about that. 'Who can tell, though I sincerely hope not. You see another problem for Mayor Feather and his mates is that I happen to be a good friend of the head of the local fire department and he knows what Feather and his mates are planning to do because I told him and he is not at all fond of what they have in mind. So I can assure you that there is no way he is going to allow some underling in his department to slip through an approval on that place without all the inspections and proper work being done to make it safe. And you know what that's going to cost them, don't you?'

'Millions,' said Hodgkiss. 'It is usually prohibitive with big old buildings like that one. I know a fellow who owned a block of four flats who was ordered to bring it up to scratch on fire safety. He had to pay massive bribes to the local fire authorities to turn a blind eye to all the problems with his building because he could never have afforded to do all the work they wanted done.'

Archer nodded. 'That's typical. And who do you think would be paying for all the work even if council ever gets it greedy paws on the old theatre. The ratepayer, that's who, and it will be Feather and his cronies who take all the profits.'

Archer continued. 'When I first heard there was a person by the name of Hodgkiss coming aboard for this production I wondered if it was you. There couldn't be too many Hodgkisses in Kanundda. I've been following your letters to the editor in the *Star* exposing council's many dodgy schemes, so if I ever need a bit of help in stopping Feather and his mates dead in their tracks over this business would you be prepared to write a few letters bringing matters to the attention of the public if I gave you the inside information on what they're doing?'

Hodgkiss frowned. He did not like the idea of writing letters to order for a stranger, not unless there was very good reason. However, Hodgkiss decided, these circumstances may well qualify as a 'very good reason.'

'I don't see why not, Archer,' he said cautiously. 'But you mustn't assume that the *Star* publishes every letter I send them. More often than not my letters get spiked.'

Here Archer nudged Hodgkiss with an elbow and rolled his eyes backward to where Chester Roberts was hovering nearby.

Archer turned. 'Well, Chester, how do you think it's going? Pleased with the way things are shaping up?'

Roberts exploded. 'Shaping up's right. All you and Victoria need is a pair of boxing gloves each then you could shape up and just get on and fight it out. Producing a play is hard enough but the two of you are not making things any easier the way you're going on.'

Archer shrugged. 'Well, there's not a lot I can do about it I'm afraid. I mean, it's not me that starts the slanging matches.'

They were interrupted by Ms Bray's hearty voice: 'Will the principals please come back on stage. I'd like to run through the murder scene in Act Three. See if we can get that nailed down.'

So Archer returned to the stage and Hodgkiss to the wings where he began to tug experimentally at the ropes he would use to operate the curtains.

Satisfied that opening and closing the curtains presented no challenges that he could not meet, Hodgkiss turned his attention to the complex diagrams to be followed for setting the stage at the beginning of each scene.

But very soon his concentration was disturbed by loud voices from the stage.

'For Chrissake don't pull the bloody thing so tight. It's quite unnecessary. I can hardly breath.'

Hodgkiss peeped around the wings. On the centre of the stage Victoria Anderson was tying Archer to a wooden chair with a length of stout rope.

'It's got to be tight or it won't look realistic,' Victoria protested, tugging heartily.

'But you don't have to get it around my neck. You bloody near choked me.'

'Quite accidental … sorry,' Victoria said without conviction. She yanked the ropes harder.

Archer squealed and started wriggling to free himself. 'Monica, if you can't control this bloody woman and stop her from assaulting me then you had better start looking for another leading man.'

'Leading man,' Victoria mocked with a nasty laugh. 'That's not what I'd call you.'

'Ladies and gentlemen please,' Ms Bray trilled. 'Enough of this badinage if you please, and Victoria perhaps not quite so much tension on the ropes if you wouldn't mind. Now, do you have the dagger handy?'

'You can count on that,' said Victoria grimly, leaning across where Archer sat, trussed and helpless, and picked up the dagger, a trick retracting model, from a small ornate side table.

'Fine,' said Ms Bray. 'Now, let's have it from the top of page seventy, if you please.'

'Then someone's going to have to untie these bloody ropes,' said Archer said between croaking gasps.

'Victoria, the ropes, please,' said Ms Bray.

'With pleasure,' said Victoria. She gave the rope a savage yank before starting to unwind it.

Hodgkiss, with an eye to remaining faithful to the script, stepped out of the wings. 'Excuse me, Ms Bray, but the dagger is supposed to be *in* the drawer of the table, not just lying around on top of it.'

Before Ms Bray could comment on this minor intervention Victoria turned towards Hodgkiss, eyes blazing. 'And who the hell do you think you are? Did you write the bloody play did you? Who gives a stuff where the bloody dagger is as long as I can get my hands on it.'

But Hodgkiss was not easily intimidated. 'The dagger has to be in the drawer because that's where the French maid put it in the previous scene. She says she didn't like the look of it and was concerned that it should be put where it can do no harm, which, of course it does.'

'Quite right, Mr Hodgkiss,' said Ms Bray. 'Thank you

very much.' She turned to Victoria. 'It will be *in* the drawer in future, Victoria, if that's where the French Maid put it. Understood. It's called continuity.'

Victoria turned an evil eye in Hodgkiss direction but declined to resume hostilities.

Having enjoyed this minor victory Hodgkiss retreated into the wings and redirected his attention to the requirements of other stage settings. In spite of his determination to concentrate on the various floor plans which he had set out on a table nearby, Hodgkiss still found himself distracted by proceedings on stage.

The dialogue, he decided, was abysmal and the manner of delivery even worse. The two principals seemed determined to prosecute their feud at any cost.

Victoria: 'Perhaps you don't you realise: I have endured as much as flesh and blood can stand.

Archer: (aside, *flesh, blood and fat in your case, my dear.*) 'Perhaps so. However it is not unreasonable to expect me to be prepared to grant some reprieve in these dire circumstances.'

Victoria: (aside, *or in your case some pretty bloody dire acting.*) 'You are such a generous soul. I am indebted to you for so long as I live.'

Archer: (aside, *which one hopes will not be too much longer.*)

Monica Bray decided it was time for a peace-making intervention. 'May we just stick to the script and forget the interesting asides if you please.'

And so a temporary truce came into force and the rehearsal proceeded.

When the run through was completed, after many pauses and further personal asides, Archer again sought out Hodgkiss in the wings.

'Another thing about the matter we were talking about

earlier. There's really a lot more to it than the problem with the fire regulations. The truth is that the mayor and his cronies have got Buckley's chance of ever doing anything with that old theatre building.'

'Oh, and why is that?' Hodgkiss asked.

Archer smiled unpleasantly and shook his head. 'The fire regulations are the least of his worries, actually. Even if Feather and McCann managed to bribe someone to get around them they'd still have a much bigger and much more expensive hurdle to jump.'

Hodgkiss nodded. 'I think I can guess what you're talking about. It's a problem common to most buildings of that age … right? You could say it is a very sick old building.'

Archer smiled approval. 'What a smart old bugger you are Hodgson. Sick. Yeah! That's a good way of putting it.'

'In fact one could almost say it is terminal depending on the degree of infection.'

'Yeah! And I've had the doctor along for a consultation and he reckons it's infected throughout. He reckons is, as you put it, terminal.'

'Bad news for the mayor then,' said Hodgkiss gathering up his diagrams of the stage settings. 'Does he know about it?'

Archer shrugged. Who knows.' He smiled unpleasantly. 'I'm certainly not going to enlighten him. See you at our next rehearsal then,' he added.

He turned to see Chester Roberts, who have been hovering nearby, disappear quickly into the wings.

Later, when the goodbyes had been said and Hodgkiss, Donald and Esme were making their way to the car park at the rear of the theatre building, Hodgkiss paused and nodded towards a large, dark sedan parked in a distant corner of the car park.

'See the fellow sitting in that car?' he said. 'Well that is none other than our patron, Kevin Feather the Mayor of Kanundda.'

'And who's the creepy little guy standing next to the car talking to him?' Donald asked.

Hodgkiss shook his head. 'I've no idea, Donald, but I can tell you one thing; I don't like being involved in anything that Feather or any of his cronies are mixed up in.'

* * *

That evening a lengthy post mortem was held in the Burke household.

Esme could not contain her disappointment at the obvious loathing that existed between the two principals.

'Why can't they just set aside their differences until the show's over. It can't be too hard surely.'

Hodgkiss grunted. 'I understand they have an interesting history; something for which she blames him and is unlikely to forgive him readily.'

'Oh yes, I've heard all about that too,' said Esme. 'But just the same, they're supposed to be adults. You have to learn to live with that sort of thing.'

'It would seem that forgive and forget are not words in either of their vocabularies. What you have on display is human nature at its worst. Two spiteful, vindictive and not over-intelligent people unable to let go of their ill-will for even a few minutes, let along a few days.'

Donald put in. 'Well, she certainly gave you a swipe of her tongue, Dad, over that business with the knife not being in the drawer. If looks could kill you'd have been stone dead. And as for learning to live with that kind of thing, well, you've never had to learn to live with it have you, Esme, and I must say that I'm surprised that you're so tolerant about the way those two were going on.'

'I'm not being tolerant at all,' Esme protested. 'I just said that you'd think that two adults would get over whatever it was that's the problem between them, even if only for a week or two until the show's over. But they don't seem to be able to do even that.'

'Then all of us will have to learn to live with it, won't we,' said Donald. 'Even the Bray woman seems to have trouble keeping them away from each other's throats.'

Hodgkiss nodded vigourously. 'Be that as it may, I can assure you that the problems that exist between those two are nothing compared with the trouble that is brewing on quite a different front.'

'And what front might that be?' Donald asked.

'The animosity that exists between Ronald Archer and those who put the money up for this production; that is the mayor of Kanundda, Kevin Feather and his cronies on council.'

'And how do they come into it?'

'I told you; they're backing this play, no doubt with ratepayers' money … your money and my money. And the reason they are backing it, or so I'm told, is solely to demonstrate what great patrons of the arts they are and that this exercise in supporting the dramatic art is nothing more nor less than a devious route to getting their greedy hands on that disused old theatre building in Robson Street. You know the one I mean?'

Esme nodded. 'You mean the old tumble-down one that's been standing empty for ages. I think that's such a shame; a lovely old building like that and it hasn't been used for a play in the last umpteen years. Remember all the shows we went to there and then that fellow who sponsored all the programmes got into some sort of trouble, didn't he, and they had to close down.'

'I don't know if "some sort of trouble" quite covers the situation, Esme. The fact is that he embezzled millions from his own business. But yes, that's the place I mean. The problem is that it doesn't meet the relevant regulations for fire safety and the work needed to bring it up to standard is horrendously costly.'

'Then how's it a problem for the council?'

'Council wants to buy it and convert it into shops and home units. But because it's an historic building they can't demolish it and start anew. However, no doubt they have devised some strategy to circumvent that problem, illegally no doubt, and have calculated that the profits they could make from a sizeable commercial development would make it well worth their while to do the work needed to meet fire regulations.'

'So that's their problem then, is it; money?' Donald asked.

Hodgkiss nodded. 'Not only money. Their first problem is that their current plan to gain approval from the fire department by bribing some local official appears to have been scotched because Archer is onto them and he's warned the head of the department of what's in the wind so that he'll be on the look-out and put a stop to any improper approvals being issued by some venal underling. But they have a much bigger problem than that; that old building is riddled with asbestos. My informant didn't tell me that in as many words, but asbestos obviously was what he was hinting at, and the cost of alleviating a problem involving asbestos dwarfs even the problems posed by the fire regulations.'

'And how do you know all this?' Donald demanded.

'I know it because for some reason best known to himself, Archer chose to confide in me. His motive in briefing me is that he hopes I will assist his campaign against the mayor by revealing these matters in letters to the editor of the *Star*.'

'You think he's just using you, then,' said Esme.

'Oh yes. He hopes to. He made no bones about it. He's noticed my previous efforts taking council to task in the letters columns of the *Star* for some of its many poor decisions in the past and assumes I would welcome the opportunity to expose more of council's foibles.'

'And would you … write letters for him.'

'No, certainly not. I would never allow myself to be used in such a fashion,' Hodgkiss said stuffily. 'But if I was convinced that there was a genuine case for bringing some improper actions of council to notice I would most certainly do my best to achieve what I thought was the proper outcome. In other words, I would do no more than my duty as a citizen.'

Esme frowned. 'Well I hope that none of this blows up before the play is over because it might make things even more awkward than they are at present.'

'Well personally I wouldn't be upset if they canned the whole show,' said Donald. He turned to Esme. 'Do you know what that cow Victoria Anderson said to me about you?'

Esme shook her head. 'No, and I'm not at all sure I want to know, thank you, Donald.'

'Of course she wants to know.' said Hodgkiss, 'but I've a feeling that you will regret raising the matter, Donald.'

Donald took the plunge. 'OK. She said the only reason you got the job was because of the size of your bust. Neither of the others who put their hands up for the part could fill out the costume. And I'll bet you had the best legs too, anyway.'

Esme did not seem at all displeased with this commentary.

'There were only two other girls put in for the part,' she said, 'but I don't think they were even asked to read the script.'

'I'm not surprised once they'd seen you,' said Donald. 'And I hope you realise the French maid actually plays an important part in the whole plot. You mightn't have that many lines to say but from what I've read of the play you've got to do a lot of things that are important in the story, like that bit where you put the knife in the drawer. Then you've got to carry that tray with the bottles that might or might not have poison in them. That's vital to the plot.'

'Really, Donald,' said Hodgkiss, 'I have no wish to detract from Esme's efforts, but the whole play verges on lunacy. The plot is so contrived and improbable that I cannot imagine that anyone who actually sees it would be able to make any sense of the action.

He continued thoughtfully. 'Why, it's so … distorted, yes, that's the word; almost as if it was written with some bizarre purpose in mind, but what that purpose is one cannot say. Perhaps time will tell.'

This piece of speculation would be vindicated soon in a most dramatic way.

* * *

The back bar of the Travellers' hotel was the favourite meeting place of those who regarded themselves as the movers and shakers of the Kanundda community.

Members of the Kanundda council and their associates, drawn chiefly from the ranks of local real estate agents and builders, were often to be found there, heads together, talking quietly and consuming round after round of drinks.

Today was a typical day.

Kanundda Mayor, Kevin Feather, was hosting fellow councillor Barry McCann, his cousin, the author Chester Roberts, and the lady responsible for the production, Monica Bray.

Also at the table, but seated a little apart, was the mayor's personal gopher, Fred Cahill.

The mayor's close acquaintances were somewhat bemused by the association that existed between the mayor and Cahill.

There were those who suspected that Cahill was a distant relation who the mayor was taking care of as a favour to someone. Others suspected that the relationship between Feather and Cahill was rather deeper and more complex than that. Some had reported claimed to have overheard Cahill speaking to the mayor in grossly disrespectful and even abusive language and the mayor had made no effort to rebuke this menial attendant and had accepted the insults offered.

But at present it was Chester Roberts who held the floor.

'Mates, we've got a problem. It's that bloody Archer bastard. He's doing everything he can to sink our project with that old theatre.'

'Yeah, tell us something we don't know mate,' said Mayor Feather. 'The smarmy bastard's been trying to make trouble for us on that front for months.'

'I know that, but this is something new, something I discovered only yesterday. He's been blowing in that bloody old Hodgkiss fellah's ear.'

Mayor Feather frowned. 'Hodgkiss? You mean that old bastard that's always writing letters to the paper attacking everything we do. And how d'you know that?'

'Because I overheard them talking about it during a break in the rehearsal yesterday.'

'And what was Hodgkiss doing at the rehearsal? Don't tell me he's actually in the play.'

Roberts shook his head. 'Not actually in the play, but someone asked him to operate the curtains. And his son-in-law, fellah by the name of Burke, he's a copper, he's mixed up in it too. He's doing the sound effects, or he's supposed to be although he made a right cock-up of it all yesterday.'

'And how on earth did they get into the act in the first place?'

Roberts shrugged. 'I've no idea.' He looked at Monica Bray. 'Do you know who invited them to come on board?'

She shrugged. 'It just came about. You know the girl who plays the French maid.'

'Girl,' McCann sneered. 'She'll never see forty again.'

'Maybe not,' said Monica. 'But she was the only reasonably presentable female who turned up when we were doing the casting. When she'd finished I told her she had the part and asked her, as I did with all the others, if she knew anyone who'd be willing to do curtains and prompt seeing we still didn't have any one. At the first rehearsal she turned up with that old Hodgkiss fellow, who's her father I think, and Burke who's her husband.'

'Gawd, you should have told us before you took them on,' said McCann.

Monica replied angrily. 'And how was I to know you lot had a problem with them. Anyway, it's too late to do anything about it now.'

'Why's that? Surely you can find some other bloke who can learn when to pull a rope at the right time and another bloke who knows how to read. We don't need mental giants here.'

'Well, Mr Mayor, I can tell you I'm sick and tired of all the brawling and back-stabbing that's been going on. I'll get rid of Mr Hodgkiss and Mr Burke as soon as you find me a couple of replacements who can do the job. Understood? And we don't have a lot of time. I'm having a full dress-rehearsal this week although God knows none of them are ready for it, particularly the two so-called leads.'

Mayor Feather nodded then turned to Fred Cahill. He said quietly: 'Right, mate. I want you to keep a sharp eye on those two, Hodgkiss and the copper, and make sure that no one gets into their ear-holes, telling them stuff they don't need to know about our plans.'

Cahill's eyes narrowed and he nodded his head slightly.

Mayor Feather turned back to Roberts. 'You were telling us about bloody Archer spilling his guts to that old Hodgkiss guy. What was he telling him?'

'Well, I didn't catch it all, but it was certainly something about the old theatre building and how we were going to convert it into flats and shops and stuff. That much I heard quite clearly.'

'And what did Hodgkiss say about it?'

'I didn't catch much of what he said because he doesn't speak so loud, but afterwards I heard Archer talking about the local rag, the *Star.* Anyway I reckon that bloody Archer is planning on getting him to write to the Star about our plans for the old theatre; the units and shops and parking and all.'

'Well that would be most unhelpful, would it?' said McCann. 'We don't need that to come out before we're good and ready to go ahead. It could stuff up everything.'

'Not wrong there,' said the mayor. 'Hodgkiss is always writing to the bloody Star getting stuck into us. Why they bother publishing his stuff I wouldn't know because it's mostly wrong.'

'Well he wouldn't be far wrong this time if he wrote what Archer's told him, would he?'

'No, so we'd better take steps to see that it doesn't

happen, right?' said Mayor Feather grimly. 'When's your next rehearsal?

'Tomorrow night,' said Roberts.

*   *   *

Ms Bray's tone was emphatically cheerful.

She stood in the middle of the brightly-lit stage, the cast and crew gathered around her.

She turned to Hodgkiss. 'I think tonight we'll have the curtains, Mr Hodgkiss … just so you can get familiar with the feel of the ropes. Did you bring a pair of gloves as I suggested? Saves the hands.'

Hodgkiss nodded. He had brought with him the pair of rubber gloves that Esme used when she did a wash-up too small for the dishwasher. He waved them in Ms Bray's direction.

'Excellent,' she said, then continued: 'And since we're still reading our parts we won't need you for prompt just yet Mr Burke so if you wouldn't mind you can do sound effects again. I still haven't managed to find anyone for that important job as yet, but I have hopes.'

She smiled and turned. 'But I *have* found someone to do our lights for us. A most important task. Please welcome Mr Cahill. Fred, isn't it.'

Cahill stepped out from the dim area at the rear of the stage, took one grudging glance around, turned and retreated out of sight.

Ms Bray called into the dark: 'Fred, do you have that script I gave you; the one with all the lighting cues marked?'

An ambiguous grunt emerged from the gloom.

Taking this for assent Ms Bray raised script. 'Now, tonight

I want to run through Act Three, Scene One once more and see if we can get this thing with the ropes and the dagger off pat. This scene is so important; the highlight of our piece. So may we have openers, please?'

Donald took his place beside the table with the assorted items for sound effects and soon found a new bell for the front door and a different gong for the clock.

At the front of the stage Hodgkiss peered around the edge of the curtain into the dark auditorium. It appeared to him sufficiently large to accommodate at least two hundred souls and under no circumstances could he imagine an audience of that size paying money to see this production.

At least the audience won't see me, he thought, relieved. Unless they make me take a curtain call at the end, but I might somehow manage not to turn up for that, he decided.

Meanwhile, on centre stage, Victoria Anderson and Ronald Archer, in their roles of Camilla and Robert respectively, had resumed hostilities.

Archer was threatening to have nothing more to do with the production unless Ms Bray could ensure somehow that his leading lady applied less vigour to the process of binding him to the chair.

Somewhere in the wings there was snigger followed by the comment: 'It's the only chance she's got to get back at him for dumping her.'

Ms Bray pretended not to hear this aside. 'I'm quite sure that Victoria will use no more force than is consistent with verisimilitude.'

'With *what*?' came the voice again, genuinely baffled.

'Now, from the beginning, please,' Ms Bray called. 'Door bell please Mr Burke.'

Donald slapped the palm of his hand down heavily on the

bell, a device similar to that to be found on the counter of many old-fashioned shops, and the action commenced.

The script required the two principals to engage in a bitter quarrel, something which required very little acting on either part.

Then Esme, in her role of French maid, answered a summons from Camilla, and crossed the stage bearing a large silver plate tray on which stood three decanters filled with water which the script said should contain fluids of various eye-catching colours and two crystal wine glasses. This she set down on a sideboard stage left and, after dropping a smart curtsy in Camilla's direction, exited the way she had come.

Archer, in his role of Robert, crossed to the sideboard, poured two drinks from one of the decanters and took them back to Camilla. They sat on a large sofa in the centre of the stage, set their drinks down on a coffee table and began an argument over how they would divide the spoils of their complicated, unlikely conspiracy.

During the course of this discussion Camilla distracted Robert's attention by inducing him to look at the clock which had just chimed. During this diversion she surreptitiously dropped some white powder into his drink.

Oblivious to this manoeuvre, Robert obligingly drank off the potion and soon became disoriented, his speech became slurred and before many minutes he had passed out. During this time Camilla kept up a non-stop monologue about what she would do with her share of the proceeds of their scam while Robert's head lolled alarmingly and appeared to fall into a sound sleep.

Camilla, believing that the potion had now taken effect, raised one of his eyelids, an examination which appeared to satisfy her that he was comatose. Having established this she began at once manfully to wrestle him from the sofa in the direction of the hard, wooden chair nearby to which, according to the script, she was to bind him.

It was obvious that Robert, far from co-operating to make his co-star's task less burdensome during this manoeuvre, was doing all he could to be difficult. His arms flopped about, managing somehow to touch Camilla in the most intimate spots; his knees gave way at the most difficult moments of the transportation; his head jerked alarmingly and when his face was turned towards the audience his eyes crossed and his tongue popped out.

But Camilla was having no more of this. She dropped him painfully mid-stage.

She turned to Ms Bray. 'I don't know how you expect me to carry that great tub of lard half way across the stage. Why can't I have that half-witted French maid to carry his feet or at least lend a hand somehow?'

But Ms Bray shook her head. 'I'm afraid the script calls for you to ...'

'Be damned to the stupid script,' Camilla shouted. 'The script calls for me to do something that could only be done my Miss American Bodybuilder so if you want someone to lug that fat oaf around the stage you can find yourself another leading lady.'

Ms Bray caved in promptly. 'Very well, Victoria, I suppose we might be able to co-opt the services of the French maid. After all, she is there to do your bidding. It's just that it could cause complications later in the plot.' She turned and called into the wings. 'What does the author think about having the French maid assist Camilla? Any complications later in the play.'

Chester Roberts's voice answered from the wings. 'Nothing that can't be sorted out with a few minor adjustments.'

'Very well, then. We'll have the French maid help carry Robert to the chair.'

'And perhaps she can help me tie him up as well,' Camilla suggested.

Again Ms Bray called off stage. 'Any objection to that Mr Roberts?'

'No. We can't have her involved in that,' Roberts called. 'It would make complications later in the plot.'

'Very well,' said Ms Bray. 'Can both principals return to the sofa and we'll take it from there … from where Robert has just gone to bye-byes. Now you, Camilla, can call for the French maid.'

Camilla turned towards the wings where the French maid had made her exit and raised both hands to her mouth, megaphone style. They she paused. 'Does the silly bitch have a name or should I just holler "French maid".'

With an effort at restraint Ms Bray suggested. 'I think it would be sufficient if you used the bell-pull to the right of the fire place. Then the French maid will come and help you.' She turned and called off-stage. 'Esme, will you be free to help?'

There was a muffled response from off stage and the scene started again. The door knocker heralded the start of the action; the bitter argument followed, the French Maid brought in the drinks, deposited them on the sideboard and made her exit; Camilla poured; the toasts were made, the white powder was introduced into Robert's glass and slumber followed.

After giving her apparently comatose co-star a contemptuous shove that nearly landed him on the boards of the stage, Camilla rose from the sofa and walked to the fire place. She raised her hand and tugged the bell rope which detached from its point and fell, settling prettily around Camilla's head and shoulders.

She swore colourfully. 'Can't anybody get anything right in this ghastly production.'

The French maid entered and the two began to wrestle with the uncooperative form on the sofa.

Again Robert's hands appeared to make accidental contact with the most intimate parts of Camilla's person while the she and the French maid attempted to move the sleeping star from the sofa to the wooden chair.

Once more Camilla dropped her co-star on the stage and outraged, turned to the director.

'If that man continues to grope me then that's the end of it as far as I'm concerned. No actress of my standing should have to put up with that sort of appalling behaviour from a creep like him.'

'Entirely accidental,' said Robert from where he sat on the stage.

'Accidental my arse,' said Camilla.

'It wasn't such a big accident as all that,' said Robert.

'Very funny, you creepy bastard. Any more of that and I ...'

But Ms Bray interrupted before the threat could be completed. 'Please. We really have to press on. So Robert, if you would please take your place in the chair and Camilla will you tie you up; this time without undue force being used if you please.

And so the rehearsal continued with less bickering. The French maid returned to the wings, Camilla bound her co-star energetically, took the retractable knife from the drawer in the table and dealt Robert his death blow by plunging it into his chest somehow avoiding the forest of ropes with which she had bound him.

The lights went out and the curtain closed quickly.

In the dark Ms Bray's voice came optimistically. 'Well,

we're getting there, aren't we?'

Hodgkiss shook his head in despair.

*   *   *

'You don't think for one moment, do you, that I will have you go on stage in front of hundreds of people wearing that?'

Donald Burke was watching in horror as his wife preened herself in front of their bedroom mirror in her French maid's costume.

'Why … why, it's positively indecent,' he spluttered.

'Nonsense, Donald,' Esme said, although privately she found the *décolletage* alarming. 'It's just a bit risqué.'

'Risqué!' he exploded. 'It leaves absolutely nothing to the imagination. You'll at least have to do something about that neckline.'

'I think she looks great,' said Hodgkiss from the doorway. 'You should be proud of her. You're a real spoil-sport, Donald. Let her have a bit of fun.'

'It's not fun, Dad. It's quite improper,' Donald said primly.

'Nonsense, Donald. She's playing the part of a French maid. She has to look a little provocative. It's traditional.'

'There's a big difference between provocative and just plain rude and that's what you look at the moment, Esme … just plain rude. Why, a woman of your age should know better.'

That put an end to any hope of an agreed settlement to the dispute.

Esme turned angrily on her husband. 'So you think a woman of my age has no business looking attractive or cute or sexy. Is that what you're saying, is it Donald? Because if that's what you mean …'

Donald held up both hands defensively. 'Honey, personally

I think you look really great. It's just that I don't like the idea of you parading yourself like that in front of strange men.'

'Oh, for heaven's sake, Donald. I'll be up on the stage and all of the strange men, as you call them, will be down in the hall in the audience miles away.'

'Not that sleazy Archer fellow,' Donald came back angrily. 'He had his hands all over Ms Anderson and I'll bet he'd've had a feel of you too if he'd had a chance.'

'He tried it on once in the dressing room,' said Esme, with a notable lack of outrage, 'and I left him in no doubt that I was not up for that sort of thing. I'd say he got the message.'

Donald's eyes popped. 'He tried to touch you in the dressing room! When was that and why didn't you tell me?'

'Because I knew exactly how you'd react … fly right off the handle. That's why I never mentioned it at the time.'

'Well that's it,' Donald said emphatically. 'That's the end of it. You're not going on.'

'Don't be ridiculous, Donald. All he did was have a feel of my bottom. It happens to all the girls.'

'Not to you it doesn't. I'm ringing that Bray woman now to let her know that neither of us will be taking ay further part in her silly little play. And I'll tell her why too.'

He reached into his shirt pocket and took out his mobile phone. 'Where did you put her number?' he demanded.

'Don't be silly, Donald. I felt flattered that he thought I was worth having a feel of. Besides, it's too late to drop out now. You'd ruin everything. It'd be too late for Monica to find replacements. It wouldn't be fair to the others. We've got our first dress rehearsal tonight don't forget.'

'Well you just stay away from that ghastly man, you hear me.'

'I can't stay away from him altogether, can I? I've got to

help Camilla, carry him from the sofa to the chair. But don't worry, Donald, I'll keep an eye out for his wandering hands. I don't want him touching me any more than you do.'

'Well you make damn sure he doesn't. The man's a grubby piece of work. And I reckon there's a warning there for you too, Dad. Remember, you told us he had plans to use you for writing letters to the paper. Well, I'd think twice before I had anything to do with him if I was you.'

'He may have plans to use me but that does not mean that I will be used. Really, Donald, I thought you'd know me better than that. I will not be used by anyone, much less a grubby specimen like Archer.'

'Well, I'm relieved to hear that. Does it mean that there won't be any letter writing?'

'It means nothing of the sort. In fact I've just had an email from him containing detailed information which, if correct, is just horrifying.'

'Horrifying,' Esme echoed. 'In what way?'

'It is horrifying in the extent of the corruption that the mayor and his cronies are prepared to engage in to make a quick buck.'

'Why, what does he reckon's going on now that he didn't tell you about before?' Donald asked.

'It appears that the fellow who originally owned the theatre also owned a large area of land on the fringe of the Kanundda Chase National Park; land that is at present zoned for open space. Well, my information from Archer is that the mayor has been in touch with the fellow's son, Brass junior, who inherited the land as well as the theatre, and he's offered to rezone at least half of this land for residential purposes if Brass will donate the theatre to council as an act charity.'

'And everybody'd live happily ever after. Is that the idea?'

'Happily and much better off, particularly a number of our local councillors who will share in the profits when the theatre is converted into shops and flats.'

'Why that's disgraceful,' said Esme. 'I can scarcely believe that people would actually do things like that.'

'It's called greed, my dear,' said Hodgkiss. 'There's a lot of it about these days, I'm sorry to say.'

'But how can you be sure that's true?' Donald asked. 'You've only got this Archer character's word for it. And as we know, he's a complete bloody sleaze-bag.'

'Being a sleaze-bag and being well-informed in matters of local corruption are two entirely different things, Donald. Personally I think he knows what he's talking about.'

'So what are you going to do about it? Write a letter to the *Star* like he asked you to?'

'That's what I'm thinking about at the moment. However, it is one thing to make an allegation on the say-so of someone who you don't really trust, but being able to prove it may not be so simple and certainly this Brass fellow, the beneficiary of the rezoning, is not likely to own up, is he?'

'He'd more likely sue you if this Archer cove has been having a lend of you and it's a lot of nonsense.'

'Yes, there is that of course. However no one has sued me so far and I think in this instance Archer is probably on the money. Nevertheless I am uneasy about it. I know I am being used and I don't like it.'

'Then don't do it, Dad,' said Esme. 'Besides, why can't he write his own letters if he's so sure of his facts? Why does he have to get you to fire his bullets?'

Hodgkiss shook his head. 'I can understand him not wanting to write the letter over his own name. That could frighten off his contacts and he appears to have one or two well-placed deep throats in the council administration. But, as I said, I have an unpleasant feeling of being used and I fear that even if I wrote the letter it may never see the light of day. And even if it *was* published it may not effect the outcome in the long run.'

Esme took her father's hand. 'Let's not talk about that any more, Dad. I want to know what you thought of my big scene. I know I wasn't actually on stage when the stabbing happened but I certainly helped with the whole business.'

'You mean your scene with Archer of the wandering hands?' said Donald.

'I think it will be quite effective on the night,' said Hodgkiss, anxious to encourage his daughter. 'A very dramatic moment ... one of the highlights of the entire drama.'

'I agree,' said Esme. 'I thought it went well. I thought that new fellow who's doing the lights, what's his name ... Fred, isn't it ... he turned the lights out at just the right moment and I thought you were good on the curtains, too, Dad; right on cue.'

'Operating the curtains is hardly a tremendously challenging task, but I suppose the timing is important if we are to make the most of that particular dramatic moment.'

Donald put in. 'Well, that Fred fellow doesn't want to turn the lights off too soon or Camilla might have trouble finding her way off the stage. As it was last night she blundered into my sound effects table and knocked everything off onto the floor.'

Hodgkiss frowned. 'But why didn't she just stay where she was until the house lights and the lights in wings came on. She would have to wait only about ten seconds or less, then she could see what she was doing and where she was going?'

'Well I'm only reporting what happened,' said Donald. 'And

of course after she'd knocked all my things over she abused me for being in her way. She's a real piece of work, that one.'

'You'll get no argument from me about that,' said Esme. 'She even had a go at me for not having my bottles or decanters or whatever you call them that I carry across to the sideboard, filled with the right stuff. "They should be full of colourful liqueurs, you stupid girl. Don't you read the script?"' she said.

'What does it say on the script?' Donald asked.

'It *does* say colorful liqueurs,' Esme conceded. 'But it wasn't even a dress rehearsal.'

'So what are you going to put in these bottles for tonight?' Donald asked.

'Decanters,' Hodgkiss corrected softly.

'Whatever,' Donald blustered.

'Well I thought I might put lime cordial in one and orange cordial in one of the others. They should be colourful enough for anyone. I haven't decided about the third one yet. Maybe blueberry or something like that.'

'Then let's hope no one actually has to drink it,' said Hodgkiss.

'I think I might put the stuff into the decanters now. I brought them home with me. Come on, Dad. You can help.'

So Hodgkiss followed Esme to the kitchen were she took a large cloth bag from under the sink, took out three antique crystal decanters and a silverplate tray. Then she opened a cupboard door above the benchtop and took down a large bottle of orange cordial and two other bottles containing blackcurrant syrup and lime cordial.

'I think these should be colourful enough for anyone, what do you think, Dad?' she asked.

'You'll water them down, won't you?' said Hodgkiss.

'Maybe a little, but I want them to be really strong colours,' said Esme. 'Now can I leave you to do that? I want to make a few adjustments to this costume before Donald has a fit.'

When Esme had gone Hodgkiss took an old blue plastic funnel from the cutlery drawer and began pouring quantities of the colourful cordials into the decanters and mixing in a little water until each of the decanters was about two-thirds full.

When he was satisfied with the result he set the decanters on the tray and holding the tray before him went in search of Esme to seek her approval.

'They're fine, Dad,' she said when he set the tray and decanters down on the dressing table in the front bedroom. 'Perfect in fact. I'd say you used a fair bit of the cordial in them.'

'Had to,' Hodgkiss confirmed, 'otherwise they would have looked anemic.'

'Well, leave them there so I won't forget to take them with me to the dress rehearsal.'

Hodgkiss nodded towards where Esme was sewing a tiny wisp of lace into the neckline of her costume. 'How's Operation Cover-Up progressing? Do you think it's enough to keep him happy?'

'I wouldn't say happy,' Esme said, holding three pins between her teeth, 'but it's as much as I'm doing. I don't want to disappoint Mr Archer too much or he might quit.'

Hodgkiss chuckled. 'Personally I thought you looked pretty good the way you were.'

Esme looked up at her father and smiled.

*　　*　　*

At last the dress rehearsal was about to get under way.

An audience of more than fifty people, friends and relatives of the players had crowded into the cold school hall and sat impatiently, talking quietly, heads together, nudging each other and poking fingers at the amateurishly printed programme which gave details of the actors and their roles and acknowledged all those working behind the scenes.

Hodgkiss, who had just finished setting the stage for the first scene, peeped out around the edge of the curtain, searching the audience in vain for a familiar face, then glanced towards the prompt box where Donald sat, hunched uncomfortably, a small but powerful light burning beside him and the script on his lap open at Act One Scene One.

Hodgkiss gave a thumbs-up sign which Donald acknowledged with a despairing shake of his head.

The recorded music, which served as the overture to the play, reached it's climax and ended with three thumping chords.

Ms Bray signaled to Hodgkiss who opened the curtains slowly, as required by his instructions.

He put his mind to attempting to watch the play as it would appear to the eyes of some disinterested spectator who was seeing the drama for the first time. But even making allowances for the occasional muffed or forgotten lines it was impossible to see how any discerning audience would be favourably impressed by the performance.

In spite of this there was laughter, generally in the appropriate places, and sometimes gasps of excitement. Surprisingly the audience seemed to be attentive and enjoying itself.

Hodgkiss thought this was very probably due to the fact that most of those in the hall would not have come to the performance with high expectations. Generally they were there to witness the efforts of some family member or friend and would therefore be more than usually forgiving.

Donald, huddled in his prompt box, was kept busy and gave the lines in a hoarse voice which, judging from reactions which Hodgkiss observed from around the edge of the curtain, appeared to carry to members of the audience in the front three rows who nodded knowingly to each other at every prompt.

Hodgkiss tried to catch Donald's attention, intending to signal that he should give the lines in a quieter voice, but Donald was frantically engrossed in following the script.

Hodgkiss, too, now busied himself in consulting the instructions for the changes to the set he would have to make at the end of the first scene which was set in a suburban sitting room. The second scene was in a business office and Hodgkiss had only two minutes to remove the sofa and armchairs and wheel a desk, chair and some bookcases into position.

Sound effects were produced on time and effectively with appropriate apparatus by a middle-aged man who Monica Bray had introduced earlier to the company as Malcolm Edwards.

The scene ended and Hodgkiss swung into action. He closed the curtains and hurried onto the stage, made the necessary changes and was back in position to receive the signal from Ms Bray to open the curtains for the next scene.

Hodgkiss noticed with some surprise that the two leads seemed to have set aside their personal animosity and were interacting as credibly as the script would permit. Others in the minor roles also were rising to the occasion.

So when the time came for the scene in which the climax of the drama was to occur, the drugging, the binding, the stabbing death of the male lead, the blackout and the quick curtain, Hodgkiss had no misgivings that the action would pass smoothly and effectively.

He noticed Esme waiting in the wings for her cue to go on stage with the decanters of coloured concoctions on the silverplate tray.

His attention switched back to the stage as he contemplated the next scene change. Then suddenly he became aware that something on the stage was wrong. Well, not exactly wrong, but different; not quite as it should be; not as he had set it at the end of the previous scene.

Yes, that was it. The plant stand with its jardinière on top was slightly out of place. He shrugged, unable to account for it but also unable to see how it would cause any problems during the action.

However, in this he was mistaken.

When Esme entered on cue the misplaced jardinière forced her to take a slightly different path across the stage towards the sideboard where she was to set down the tray.

This new path took her across a badly worn Turkey rug that was ruffled at the edges. Esme stumbled, one of the decanters fell from the tray and crashed to the floor. The stout crystal of the decanter withstood the fall, but the stopper fell out.

Hastily Esme stooped, replaced the stopper, returned the decanter to the tray and continued across the stage to the sideboard where she set the decanters down.

The two principals suspended their scripted bickering and Camilla turned to Esme and *ad libed:* 'Clumsy, stupid girl. You can take a fortnight's notice.'

Esme appeared suitably chastened and departed the stage, head down in disgrace.

Minutes later she had to answer Camilla's summons and return to the stage to assist in transporting the comatose hero from the sofa to the chair where he was to be bound, then depart off stage once more.

Once in the wings she hurried to where Hodgkiss stood, his hands gloved, ready for the quick curtain.

'Someone moved that ruddy pot plant thing,' Esme hissed.

'I noticed that just before you went on,' said Hodgkiss, *sotto voce*. 'Have you any idea who might have moved it and why.'

Esme shook her head and muttered; 'I'd like to get my hands on whoever did it because it made me go out of my way and stumble over that silly rug.'

They both turned to watch the stage where Camilla was binding Robert to the chair. The ropes were being tied vigourously but Robert remained unresisting, slumped limp against the back of the chair.

Camilla reached across the recumbent form, pulled open the small drawer in the table beside the sofa, took out the retractable knife, raised it dramatically over her head and plunged it down into the body which heaved convincingly then became still.

The lights went out immediately and Hodgkiss began pulling quickly on the ropes. The curtain closed with a satisfactory swing.

That should have given them a cheap thrill for their money, he thought, then, upon reflection decided that this audience of favoured friends of the cast probably had been admitted gratis.

Well, admitted free or not, they were showing their appreciation by sustained clapping and stamping of feet.

Then Hodgkiss heard Ms Bray's hushed but penetrating voice from the darkened wings. 'Well done, company. Well done.' Then: 'Lights please, Mr Cahill.'

At once the lights in the wings came on.

On stage Camilla was standing over the slumped body of her male lead.

'Will someone come and help me untie him? He's being his usual silly uncooperative self.' Then, after a short silence, urgently. 'Please someone come here quickly.'

In his cramped box at the front of the stage Donald recognised the panic in the actress's voice. He scrambled awkwardly up onto the stage and hurried to where Camilla stood leaning over Robert who was still sitting slumped and trussed to the wooden chair.

Aware of Donald beside her Camilla turned: 'Something's wrong. The knife ... it's gone. It was supposed to stay stuck on.' She looked about the stage. 'It's not here.'

She stooped, seized Robert by the shoulders and began shaking him vigourously. 'Come on, you silly fool, stop pretending and help me untie these silly ropes.'

But Robert's only response was for his head to loll from one side to the other.

Donald said quietly, indicating the front of Robert's clothes: 'I'd say that's blood. Did you use some sort of fake blood?'

'No, of course not,' she said sharply. 'There was no need for that because the lights went out straight away.' Then she leaned down to make a closer examination of Robert's chest area. 'Blood! But you're not serious.'

'I'm afraid I am.' Donald turned to the front of the stage and called: 'Dad, would you come here. Hurry please.'

Hodgkiss emerged from the wings at the front of the stage and hurried across.

Donald had his hand on the side of Robert's throat. He turned as Hodgkiss approached.

'This man is dead,' he said quietly. 'I want you to stay right here and don't let anybody come near him or touch anything on this stage. Right?'

Hodgkiss nodded and Donald, followed by Camilla, walked

towards the wings where the company was gathered in a small group looking anxiously out onto the stage.

Monica Bray stepped forward. 'Is something wrong? What's happened to Mr Archer?'

Donald shepherded Ms Bray back into the wings taking his mobile phone from his shirt pocket as he did so and thumbing the keypad.

He turned to face the group. 'I'm sorry to have to tell you that Mr Archer has died and I am not at all satisfied about the circumstances. So I am going to ask for support to enable a thorough investigation to begin. Therefore I want you all to remain here in the wings for the time being. I have asked Mr Hodgkiss to stay there on stage to make sure that nothing is touched or interfered with in any way. I have no doubt that this is a crime scene. Also, Ms Bray, I want you to take whatever steps are necessary to make sure that we have particulars of all the people in the audience out there tonight.'

Ms Bray replied anxiously: 'I think we know everyone in the house tonight. They were all here by invitation.' She turned to the company. 'That's so, isn't it? It was all friends and family.'

Everyone nodded shocked agreement.

'Nevertheless they must stay where they are until police arrive to take their names and addresses. I'll let them know that the show will not be continuing and that they will have to wait.'

'Are you going to tell them why?' asked Victoria Anderson, abandoning her plumy Camilla voice.

'Not in any detail,' said Donald waiting for his call to be answered.

Then he conducted a hush conversation into his tiny phone, cut the connection and returned it to his pocket.

While Donald was busy on his phone Hodgkiss wandered

upstage then explored the dim area behind the flies. His feet encountered some gritty substance and her stooped, wet a finger, dabbed it at the dark floorboards then raised it for inspection.

Sand, he decided. He had trodden in a small patch of sand. Now, why would there be sand in this remote spot in the old building.

Meanwhile Donald had finished his call. He returned the phone to his pocket and turned to the hushed group waiting in a semi-circle in the wings.

He asked: 'Did any of you notice anything at all out of the ordinary tonight?'

Baffled heads where shaken silently.

'Everything happened exactly as it should have,' Monica Bray said, then added, 'surprisingly.'

'But the knife,' Victoria Anderson protested, a note of hysteria in her voice. 'What's happened to the knife? The plastic one. It was supposed to stay there, sticking in his chest. And I couldn't possibly have hurt him … not with that. It couldn't possibly have made him bleed. It was plastic for God's sake and the blade was designed to retract.'

'Don't worry, Ms Anderson,' said Donald, 'we'll find the knife. I'm more interested in the other knife. The one that killed him. It wasn't plastic.'

'But it's not possible,' said Ms Anderson. 'The whole thing's not possible. I stabbed him with a plastic knife. I distinctly heard him say: "you didn't have to whack me like that. It hurt." Then the lights went out and the curtain closed.'

'And you stayed right where you were, did you?' Donald asked.

'Yes of course I did. It was pitch black and I didn't want to trip over something like that silly girl did.'

Esme snorted. 'It wasn't my fault. Someone moved that pot plant arrangement and I had to take a detour over that wrinkly old rug. If it hadn't been for that ...'

'It would never have happened if you'd looked where you were putting your great hoofs,' Victoria snapped.

'OK, that's enough of that,' said Donald. 'I'll want statements from all of you about what you were doing during the few minutes before and after the lights went out.'

'But we were all just standing in the wings,' said Jefferson, the police inspector.

Donald shook his head. 'That's simply not true, Mr Jefferson' said Donald. 'I, for one was not standing in the wings. Nor was Mr Hodgkiss. Nor was the gentleman who operated the lights. And you, Mr Jefferson, while it's true you were standing in the wings you were in the wings on the opposite side of the stage to most of the others because that's where you make your entry in the next scene.'

Donald looked about to make his point. 'So it's not so simple as everyone being in the wings. Now, I think that sounds like my back-up team arriving. If you'll all just stay exactly where you are I'll be right back.'

Donald disappeared through the curtains. Minutes later he returned with a large police officer in full uniform.

'This is Superintendent O'Hare,' he announced, 'and there is a number of constables on standby in the auditorium and a police doctor will be here any minute.'

The police doctor, a short, jolly man, arrived almost at once. He swept the curtains aside and made his entry with flair, black bag in hand. He greeted Donald, introduced himself as Roger Ferris, and Donald, rather unnecessarily, pointed out the body.

'Well, he's not going anywhere, is he, all trussed up like

that,' said Doctor Ferris, cheerfully. 'Now let's have a look what's wrong with him.' He turned to Donald. 'I'll have to untie him first.' He began to undo the ropes with some difficulty. 'Whoever tied him up certainly made a good job of it,' he commented.

In the wings Victoria Anderson smiled proudly.

It did not take Dr Ferris long to discover the source of the blood staining the ropes that had bound Archer to the chair.

'Narrow penetrating wound to the heart,' he announced. 'Very neatly done. Trussed up like that he couldn't have done it himself so you'll have to look elsewhere for the culprit, eh? Done very recently too.'

'We know when it was done, Doctor. What sort of weapon would have done it?'

'Any narrow blade six inches long would have done the trick,' he said. He nodded towards the wings where the company stood, still awestruck. 'I see you have a selection of suspects. My wife does the odd bit of amateur theatricals and if what she tells me about the jealousy and back-stabbing that goes on among thespians I'd say you'll have no trouble finding someone with a motive, or perhaps plenty of people with motives. Can I take him now? I'll do the PM first thing tomorrow and send you a report, but it won't tell you anything I haven't already told you.'

Dr Ferris strode across to the curtains, parted them deftly and signaled to the auditorium. Moments later two men bearing a stretcher stepped out of the wings onto the stage, lowered Archer's body from the chair onto the stretcher and disappeared into the wing, the corpse slung between them.

All heads turned to follow this melancholy procession then Donald and Superintendent O'Hare held a whispered consultation.

The superintendent turned to the waiting company. 'There are two constables waiting in the hall. I want each of you to make a statement to them about your movements tonight then you are free to go home.'

Donald nodded gloomily. 'I've got a bad feeling about this one, boss,' he said quietly to the superintendent. 'They're a weird collection of people, these actors and actresses. You wouldn't know who was doing what half the time because everyone would have been looking at what was happening here on stage. And the lights were down dim for much of the time so you couldn't see much going on in the wings anyway.'

He shook his head. 'I don't like it at all.'

'What about Edgar?' the superintendent asked. 'Have you asked him if he noticed anything strange going on? You know he doesn't miss a trick.'

Donald frowned. 'I don't think the Oracle of Lillimoor is going to be able to help us with this one. He was stuck down in front there opening and closing the curtains. I'd say he had his hands full too, with that and changing the scenery, to have noticed anything much.'

'But you will ask him, won't you, Donald?' the Superintendent insisted.

'Oh I'll ask him all right, don't worry about that, but as I said, I don't hold out much hope for him this time.'

'Well, if he runs true to form he'll have noticed something that's going to help us sort it out,' said Superintendent O'Hare confidently.

Donald frowned and looked to where his father-in-law was standing in the wings, hand raised thoughtfully to his well-trimmed grey beard.

*   *   *

'Is it true. Bloody Archer's dead?'

Mayor Feather could scarcely contain his glee.

Seated opposite, across the mayor's wide desk, Cr McCann nodded. 'That's what I heard. My nephew was in the audience at the dress rehearsal. After the big scene where Archer's supposed to get murdered everything came to a halt and then the coppers arrived. Everyone in the audience had to wait around for a bit while the cops made sure of their names and addresses and he heard one of the cops telling another cop that the guy that was supposed to get stabbed on stage had actually been stabbed in real life and that he was a goner. Or that's what he heard.'

'But there's no doubt he's dead, is there?'

'No. It was all over the radio this morning: "Actor killed in murder scene on stage. Police baffled," they said.'

'And wasn't there a copper actually in the play?' Mayor Feather asked.

McCann shook his head. 'No, not in the play. He was doing prompt.'

'Oh yes, I remember. You told me. He reads the lines to the actors when they forget. Sounds hopeless to me. So where does this leave us. No one can bring any of this back to *us*, can they?'

'Why would they be able to do that? We had nothing to do with it ... did we?'

'Nah. Of course not.'

'What about that gopher fellow of yours, Fred Cahill. He was in this play too, wasn't he? What's he told you about it? He was there ... must have been.'

'Yeah. He was there ... doing the lighting. Just turning the lights on and off at a switchboard at the back of the building. Nothing to do with the actors.'

McCann looked hard at the mayor. 'You sure he didn't do something he shouldn't've. He's a weird little guy.'

'Hey, steady on there; he's a relation of the wife. Cousin or something.'

'Makes no difference whose relation he is. Anyway, Archer's dead now and I can't think of too many people who'll miss him. Arrogant little bastard he was from all accounts. So where do we stand now with young Brass and the old theatre building? We don't have to worry any more about the late Mr Bloody Archer telling people about the asbestos problem there.'

'One hundred percent right, mate. You know something; I was wondering if young Mr Brass knows about that asbestos in his old theatre. His old man probably knew about it before he kicked the bucket, but even so it's not something he'd want to talk about; not something you want everyone knowing about because of what it does to the value of the property. I mean who wants to own a building that's full of bloody asbestos, right?'

McCann smiled. 'Hey, you're on to something there, mate. If Brass doesn't know about the asbestos it'll be a very nasty surprise and he might be only too pleased to get out of it quick smart for less than he's asking at present. I mean, ask yourself: what's worse than owning an old theatre building that no one can use because of the fire regulations? The answer is: owning an old theatre building that no one can ever use until you've got rid of all the asbestos. I reckon if I owned a building like that and I had a potential buyer waiting in the wings so to speak, I'd be tempted to practically give the thing away. Talk about a white elephant.'

'Yeah, and there's something else going our way in this transaction. I was talking to Brass a few days ago. Did you know you know his old man owned some open space land adjoining Kanundda National Park out the end of St James? Now, of course, he owns it.'

McCann shook his head. 'First I've heard about it.'

'Well, he was asking me quite casually what's the chance of it being rezoned for residential?'

'Of course you told him it's not on, right? I mean the guy's rich enough without us presenting him with a couple of million dollars more by opening up his land for housing development.' He paused. 'Unless, of course ...'

Mayor Feather smiled. 'Exactly. Unless of course he gave us the theatre.'

'And cleaned up the asbestos first.'

'Yeah. And fixed the fire regulation problem.'

'This land of his would need to be worth big bickies to cover the cost of all that work.'

'It is. No mistake. He's got enough land to chop it up into a hundred blocks even after building the roads. He'd make millions out of it and be miles ahead even if he had to fix up the old theatre for us.'

'Hey, did Archer know about this land the Brass boy owns and how he wants a deal?'

Mayor Feather shrugged. 'Who knows? And now, who cares. If Archer told someone what can they do with it? He couldn't have had any idea that Brass'd talked to me about it. It would only have been scuttlebutt. Nothing reliable. I mean, that Archer guy was full of bullshit.'

'So it's steady as she goes, is that how you see it?'

'That's exactly how I see it. Steady as she goes. And I'll be having another talk to young Brass soon about his land and what sort of a deal he could do. I take it you're still on board.'

'What do you think?! There's enough money in that old theatre for all of us once we get it fixed and I reckon Brass will be anxious to get rid of it if he can do a deal with us on that land of his.'

There was a knock on the door and Fred Cahill came in with a large package. 'Special delivery, boss,' he announced. 'Guy dropped it off at the counter downstairs.'

The mayor turned. 'Put it on my desk, Fred,' said the mayor.

'Bit of excitement at the playhouse last night, Fred?' McCann asked.

Cahill turned to look at him but said nothing.

'Fellow died, didn't he?' McCann continued.

Cahill nodded slowly. 'Yeah. That's right. He died.'

'But someone helped him, no?'

'I wouldn't know anything about that. I wasn't there at the time.'

'Not there?' asked McCann, surprised. 'I thought you were doing the lights for this Mickey Mouse production.

'Yeah. That's right. But I wasn't where it happened. That was on the stage. I never went on the stage.'

McCann nodded. 'Sure. I understand.' He looked at the mayor who was watching him, frowning, tight lipped.

*   *   *

'You know I shouldn't have shown you those statements. You've got no right to see any of them.'

Sitting opposite his father-in-law at the round red wood table on the back deck of the Burke's home, Donald watched uneasily as his father read carefully through the statements taken from those in the school hall at the time of Archer's death.

'Don't worry, Donald,' said Hodgkiss without looking up. 'I won't tell anybody. Besides, Superintendent O'Hare said it was all right to show them to me, didn't he?'

Donald said nothing. Then: 'Well, what have you learned that you didn't already know … if anything?'

'I have learned that people generally are not at all observant and that unless you question them about something they rarely make an effort to search their minds for details.'

He continued: 'I assume you just let these people sit down somewhere by themselves and write out these useless documents.'

'That's the way it's done, Dad.'

'Then all I can say is that it's no wonder that you so often find yourself in need of some external assistance.'

Donald inhaled deeply but offered no comment.

Hodgkiss asked. 'I assume you still have no idea where the missing knives are?'

Donald shook his head.

Hodgkiss continued: 'Have you formed any idea about why it may have been necessary for the murderer to remove the plastic knife before committing his crime?'

'Perhaps it was in the way,' said Donald without any conviction. 'Don't forget that Archer had all those ropes tied around him, particularly around his chest and that's where the fake plastic knife was stuck. I'd say the killer pulled it off so he had a clear go at stabbing Archer between the ropes.'

Hodgkiss paused: 'I have grave difficulty in understanding why neither of those knives has been found. I take it everybody on the stage at the time was searched thoroughly before they were allowed to leave?'

'Of course they were.'

'And have you explored the possibility that one of them could have somehow passed one or both of the knives to someone in the audience so they could dispose of them when they left.'

Donald shook his head. 'Everybody in the audience was searched too before they were allowed to go home. But I don't see how someone in the cast could have got hold of them and smuggled them to someone in the audience. It wouldn't have been possible. I mean, you were there. In fact I put you on guard on the stage immediately after we realised the guy was dead specially to make sure that nothing of that sort happened.'

Hodgkiss nodded agreement. 'Then they must be somewhere in the hall, mustn't they, Donald.'

Donald shrugged. 'If they are then we haven't been able to find them.'

Hodgkiss offered no comment and returned his attention to the statements.

When he had finished reading the last statement he returned the bundle to large manila envelope then looked up and asked sharply: 'There was no mention anywhere of the sand. Why not?'

Donald looked up, mouth open. 'Sand! What sand? What are you talking about, Dad?'

'There was sand on the floor towards the back of the stage. I trod in it. There is no mention of that in any of the statements. I would like to know why.'

'I'd say that's because no one noticed it.'

'Your officers were supposed to make a thorough search of the building, were they not? How could they not notice it? I noticed it in two minutes while you were on the phone to ask for back-up.'

'OK. So you trod in some sand. Why's that a big deal?'

'It is a big deal because it has not been accounted for. I do not believe for one minute that your officers who searched the building could have failed to notice it, but for some reason they have not mentioned it in their statements nor has any of the company.'

'I suppose no one mentioned it because no one thought it was important … that is no one except you. So you reckon it's important, do you?'

'Really, Donald, I have no idea if it is important or not and I won't until I know where it came from and how it got there.'

'And how do you propose to do that?'

'By making an inspection of the area, that's how.'

Donald sighed. 'An inspection of the area, eh?' he repeated lamely. 'Well, let's do it now … get it out of the way.'

He rose and without a word headed for the shallow flight of wooden steps leading down from the back deck to the driveway where the unmarked police car stood.

Hodgkiss followed and climbed into the front seat beside Donald. The short trip to the school was passed in an uncomfortable silence.

Once inside the hall Hodgkiss mounted the steps to the stage, parted the curtains and held them back for Donald to follow.

'Now, where's all this famous sand?' Donald asked.

Hodgkiss pointed towards the rear of the stage.

It took no time at all to find it.

'There's not a lot of it,' said Donald looking down at the small patch of white sand.

'Too much to have come in on someone's shoes,' said Hodgkiss.

Hodgkiss headed off towards the rear of the building, head down, searching in the gloom.

But it was Donald who found the source of the sand.

'Here you are, Dad,' he called. 'Here's where your mysterious sand came from.'

Hodgkiss hurried over and saw a sandbag with a gash in the side leaning against the back wall of the theatre. A small heap of sand had leaked out. Two similar bags lay nearby. These appeared intact.

'I think they use these bags as counter-weights in scenery changes, don't they?' Donald asked.

Hodgkiss nodded. 'That answers one of our questions; where did the sand come from? The next questions to be answered are why was the bag slashed and how did the sand get from the bag to the spot where we found it on the back edge of the stage area.'

Donald shook his head. 'Is that all. I thought you might find more questions to ask,' he said sarcastically.

'Of course I have more questions to ask and the first one is to you, Donald.'

'Oh, and what might that be, although I know I'll regret asking it.'

'It is simply this: why are you not in the least bit curious about it?' Hodgkiss asked, stooping to examine the tiny deposit of white sand at the rear edge of the stage area.

'That's an easy one. I'm not particularly curious about your little patch of sand because I don't see how it can have anything to do with how or why that guy got killed … and I reckon you can't either, right?'

Hodgkiss nodded. 'You're correct, Donald I can't either, but I intend to find a reason; a connection between the sand and Mr Archer's very timely death.'

'Very timely!' said Donald, surprised. 'What's so timely about it?'

'Have you forgotten what Archer told me about Mayor Feather's plans to acquire that old theatre building?'

Donald laughed. 'Oh come off it, Dad. Are you trying to

tell me that this is somehow tied up with all that stuff he told you about council buying the old theatre?'

'I suppose you regard that as entirely irrelevant, do you?'

'Well I reckon it's a bit far-fetched to try and tie the mayor in with this business.'

'But the mayor is already tied in with it. The author of the play, Chester Roberts, is a friend of the mayor; the director, Monica Bray is also a friend of his and the man who operated the lights, Fred Cahill is an employee of the mayor. I'd say that ties Mayor Feather quite firmly to the matter, wouldn't you, Donald?'

Donald shrugged. 'Maybe. But I still don't see what the sand's got to do with it.'

'No, I dare say not. May we go home now, Donald. I have some thinking to do.'

*　*　*

'What are you doing there, Dad?' Esme asked, then added: 'Aren't those all the plans for the stage sets?'

Hodgkiss looked up from the redwood table on the back deck where he had set out the floor plans for the stage sets for each scene of the now-abandoned production.

When her father failed to respond Esme walked around the table and sat down on the curved bench opposite. 'I thought the whole the play had been called off.'

'And so it has,' said Hodgkiss.

'Then why are you looking at those old floor plans for the sets? Nobody's going to need them any more, are they?'

'I need them, Esme. The play may have been cancelled but the murder investigation has not and I suspect that Donald's inquiries are going nowhere fast at present and he will shortly be looking to me for some assistance.'

'And you think you can help him by looking at those old plans showing where all the furniture and things should be in each scene of the play. How's that going to help him?'

'I don't know … yet,' said Hodgkiss, his patience wearing thin.

'And what exactly are you looking for … what do you hope to find?'

'Anomalies. That's what I hope to find. And I'm more likely to find them if I am left in peace to concentrate on what I'm doing.'

'All right, Dad. No need to get shirty about it. I can take a hint. I just thought I might be able to help. I still don't see what you can find out just by looking at them,' she said gesturing to the plans set out on the table.

His concentration now broken, Hodgkiss looked up. 'Nor do I, Esme. In fact it is quite likely that I will learn nothing whatever from them, but we do not have a great deal to go on at the moment.'

'I realise that Dad,' said Esme. 'That's why I want to know if there's anything I can do to help? If Donald is getting nowhere, as you seem to think, perhaps you and I should work together to help him. Haven't you got any idea at all about who might have done it … and how? Have you thought about who had the means, the motive and the opportunity. You and Donald always talk about how finding out those three things is the way to go about an investigation.'

Hodgkiss nodded, smiling. 'Quite right, my dear. And of course there's the other question: who benefits? That's usually an important factor.

'Now, if we look at motive first there is a pretty wide field which includes anyone connected with council's scam relating to the old theatre they are hoping to acquire.

'And of course that also helps us to answer the question of who stands to benefit from Archer's death.

'The question of opportunity is the biggest problem.

'The means of course is the knife the killer used and which we have not yet been able to locate, although there is some reason to believe that it is still in the theatre.

'Then there is also the question of why did the killer remove the plastic retractable knife from the scene of the crime. Once he removed it from Archer's body he could have just left it lying on the stage. Why did he not do so?'

'Fingerprints, of course,' said Esme.

Hodgkiss nodded. 'That is certainly the most obvious explanation.'

'Which means that he wasn't wearing gloves, doesn't it?'

Again Hodgkiss nodded. 'And perhaps he wasn't wearing gloves because if he had been anyone who saw him may have remembered it and wondered why.'

'So you think it was one of the cast?'

'One of the cast or that fellow who was roped in to do the sound effects, what was his name, I've forgotten.'

'Malcolm Edwards. He's a friend of Ms Bray.'

'Yes, him, or that other chap; the one who did the lights, Fred Cahill.'

'Yes,' said Esme thoughtfully. 'I never liked him. There's something really creepy about him.'

'No argument there, my dear. And he's very thick with the mayor so he should be near the top of our list of suspects.'

'Now, what about opportunity?' said Esme. 'Cahill didn't have much opportunity, did he?'

Hodgkiss nodded. 'Perhaps less opportunity than some of the others who were nearer. And we must not forget Malcolm Edwards. Where did Ms Bray find him? Is he a mate of the mayor? And of course the one with the most opportunity was Victoria Anderson ... Camilla. She was right there, on the spot. She could have done the stabbing all right. She could have concealed the real knife in her clothes then stabbed him with it after the lights went out and after she had stabbed him with the fake knife.'

'Yes, but how did she get rid of both knives.'

Hodgkiss shook his head. 'That, of course, is the problem with all of the suspects. How did they get rid of the murder weapon and the fake knife? They must be somewhere in the hall still because, according to Donald, everyone was thoroughly searched before they left, including those in the audience.'

He sighed. 'You know this whole thing has been a worry right from the start.'

'A worry? In what way?'

'Well, first of all there's the play itself. I mean, my dear, you have to admit it is an awful piece of work. So awful in fact that it made me wonder whether or not it been written specially to create a scenario for a real murder to be committed. I think that is a possibility and therefore I intend to recommend to Donald to have a very serious discussion with the fellow who wrote it, Chester Roberts – a well-known friend of the mayor – to ask whence his inspiration came.'

'That's pretty way-out, isn't it, Dad? I mean writing the play to order so you could actually murder one particular character?'

'Perhaps, Esme, perhaps, but I believe it is a worthwhile line of inquiry and I shall certainly recommend to Donald that he pursue it.'

'Well, I don't know if he'll take too kindly to that.'

Hodgkiss shrugged. 'I can't be worried about that.

Meanwhile, if you will leave me in peace I will resume my perusal of these plans of the stage settings for each scene. Then, of course, there is the business of the sand.'

'What sand is that?' Esme asked.

'Didn't you know? There were several sandbags at the back of the stage. One of them had been slashed open and there was a small scattering of sand near the back of the stage, a little mystery in itself.

'And no one seems to have attached any importance to it.'

'But you do, do you, Dad?'

'I certainly feel it should be accounted for in some way.'

'And you think you can account for it by going over the plans for the stage settings.'

'Not necessarily, but something may occur to me.'

'Or it may not,' said Esme, pushing back the bench and rising. 'I'll bring you out some sandwiches in ten minutes. OK?'

'Thank you, Esme.'

'Something may have occurred to you by then perhaps.'

'Perhaps.'

After his daughter had disappeared through the heavy sliding doors to the family room Hodgkiss resumed his examination of the plans.

Ten minutes later Esme returned with a plate of cheese and tomato sandwiches in one hand and a mug of hot black tea in the other.

'Well, did you find it; this anomaly.'

Hodgkiss looked up. 'Perhaps. When I've finished these sandwiches will you kindly drive me to the school.'

'Why? Do you want to have another look around that hall?'

'Only the stage. Not the hall.'

Esme shook her head. 'I can't do that unless Donald says it's all right.'

'It'll be fine with Donald,' said Hodgkiss taking a bite from one of the sandwiches. 'I'm only asking you to do this so I can help with his investigation.'

'Well that may not be how he sees it. He might think you're just interfering.'

Hodgkiss shook his head. 'Esme, how often has my so-called "interfering" resulted in Donald solving a case?'

'Look, you don't need to convince me about that, Dad. But you know how sensitive Donald is sometimes about the way you go about helping him.'

'Esme, if you do not wish to take me just say so and I will make other arrangements since what I plan to do is a matter of some importance. If necessary I will resort to calling a cab.' Hodgkiss knew his daughter's views on using cabs when there was a perfectly good family car in the garage.

Esme snapped. 'You'll do nothing of the sort. Just finish your sandwiches then I'll take you. But I think we should let Donald know.'

'No time for that. Speed is of the essence. Those responsible may even now be attempting to cover their tracks.'

'Cover their tracks. So who do you think might have tracks to cover; who are "those responsible" you mentioned?'

'There will be plenty of time to discuss that after we visit the hall and I have some hard evidence to support my theory … not before.'

Esme sighed. 'All right, Dad. Come on then.'

Hodgkiss wolfed down the remaining sandwich then swilled down his tea. 'I'm ready to go,' he announced.

But when they arrived at the school a young constable was standing on guard at the entry to the hall.

When they approached he introduced himself as Constable Cullen. 'I'm sorry, Mrs Burke,' he said after Hodgkiss had introduced Esme and himself and explained the purpose of their visit, 'but I can't let you into the hall. Not without permission from Inspector Burke. Do you want me to ring him?'

Finally, after Esme had spoken to him on the phone at some length, Donald relented.

'And whatever your father expects to find there after half the New South Wales police force has been over it umpteen times I can't imagine,' he told her, then asked her to hand the phone back to the constable so he could give the necessary authority for them to enter the hall.

Inside the hall Hodgkiss made his way up onto the stage, Esme hard on his heels and with Constable Cullen following, ready to enforce Donald's instructions that his father-in-law should do nothing to contaminate the crime scene.

Standing in the middle of the stage Hodgkiss looked about then took out of his slacks pocket one of the plans for a stage setting.

'What have you got there, Mr Hodgkiss?' the constable inquired.

'This, Constable Cullen,' Hodgkiss explained, 'is the plan for the stage setting for the scene in which the murder took place.' He unfolded it and held it out. 'You will see that it shows in diagrammatic form the position of all the stage properties used in the scene including this couch where the male and female leads sat and had one of their many acrimonious disagreements. It was during this time that the drug which Camilla, the female lead, had administered in a drink to her co-star, Robert, took effect.

'Then when Robert had passed out Camilla, with the assistance of the French maid, played by my daughter here, Esme, carried him with great difficulty and little cooperation to this wooden chair near the sofa.

'The positions of both the couch and the chair are shown clearly on my map of the stage.

'Once Robert was rather precariously installed in the wooden chair the French maid exited stage right and Camilla began to bind her victim with a stout rope.

'When she had finished tying him up she reached across to the little table located near the couch,' he pointed to the spot on the plan, 'took a knife from the drawer and dispatched her tormentor.

'To heighten the effect of this piece of drama the lights were immediately extinguished and the curtain closed very rapidly and, may I say, very efficiently by yours truly.

'There followed a period of about fifteen seconds when the lights were out both on the stage and in the hall.

'In other words there was near total darkness.

'During this time there was sustained applause from the audience because it was the end of the act and they obviously had appreciated the high drama of the moment.

'The question is: where was everyone while the lights were out?

'We know that Camilla, or Victoria Anderson, was still on stage although she had moved a short distance in the direction of the wings from where she had been standing by the wooden chair when she stabbed her victim. She claimed in her statement that she was afraid to go any further towards the wings for fear of tripping over something or someone or bumping into something or someone.

'Credible enough, I suppose.

'However, one thing is fairly certain; if she *is* the killer she would have had little opportunity to dispose of the knives.

'Everyone else in the company has said that they remained in their positions from the time the blackout started until the main lights in the auditorium came on and the lights came on in the wings and on the stage.

'But of course we have only their words for that and we can believe them or not.

'The killer obviously is lying. Proving that may prove difficult, but I believe there are some indications that may help us understand what happened.'

'"Indications"? Clues, you mean?' said Esme.

'Yes, I suppose you could call them clues. The first clue is apparent on this plan for the positions of the stage properties at the beginning of this scene in which the murder took place.'

Hodgkiss set down the plan on the table containing the drawer from which Camilla had taken the plastic knife. The other two huddled around him.

'So what're these clues?' Esme asked.

Hodgkiss put a finger on the plan. 'That's one.'

They all looked at where Hodgkiss's finger rested on the plan then at the corresponding point on the stage where the plant stand stood towards the back of the set with a jardinière resting on top.

'How's that a clue?' Esme asked.

The constable said: 'I may be wrong, Mr Hodgkiss, but I'd say that whoever drew the position of that plant stand on your plan drew it at a different time to the rest of the things; the couch, the table, the chair and the sideboard, because it's drawn in ink while the positions of the other things are all in pencil.'

Hodgkiss nodded, smiling. 'You're quite right, Constable. Well spotted.'

'Then who drew it on the plan and why?' Esme asked.

'I drew it on later than the other items for the simple

reason that the plant stand with its jardinière were not part of the original stage set when we started rehearsals. It did not appear on the set until the third rehearsal. That's when I drew it in on my plan of the set for that scene.'

'But who put it on the set? I mean, did it just appear out of the blue?'

'Yes, it did … or seemed to. Naturally I asked the director, Ms Bray, about it and she was completely at a loss to explain why it was there or who had asked for it to be put it there.

'Then she made inquiries among the others and finally Chester Roberts, the author of the play, admitted that he had arranged for it to be included in the stage props for that scene.'

'But why? And why put it there, on that particular spot?'

'Ms Bray told me that Roberts had told her he thought it helped to dress the stage up … make it more like a living room.'

'Well, I don't think it dresses up the stage at all,' said Esme. 'I mean it's just a pot on a pillar. It doesn't even have any flowers in it. It's just empty except for a bit of sand in the bottom. I know that because I looked in it when it first turned up. And not only that, it caused my accident with the decanters because it was in my way and I had to walk around it and across that silly rug that was all creased up, making me trip.'

Constable Cullen pointed to the plan. 'According to that it's still not in the right spot, is it? According to where you've marked it on the diagram it should be further to the right from where we're standing now … more towards the wings.'

Hodgkiss nodded. 'Well done again, Constable. It is certainly not in the correct spot and I can demonstrate that it has been moved because when it first appeared on the set I marked its correct spot in chalk with an X on the stage so I would know exactly where to place it when I changed the scene.'

Esme and the constable followed Hodgkiss as he headed to where the plant stand stood at the rear of the set. Hodgkiss stooped and pointed to a small X written on the boards in faint blue chalk.

'It's about three feet away from where it should be,' Esme commented.

Hodgkiss nodded. 'Now, why is that? Does anyone have a theory?'

'Perhaps you simply put it in the wrong spot, Dad, when you were changing the set at the end of the previous scene.'

Hodgkiss shook his head vigourously. 'No, Esme. I put it on its correct spot. I had a torch so I could see exactly where to place it and I am in no doubt that I put it on its correct spot; on the X. Any other ideas?'

Esme frowned. 'If that's so then it means that someone must have moved it during the scene. But that's just not possible, is it, because someone would have been sure to notice? Which means that whoever moved it must have moved it just moments after you finished setting the stage for the new scene – the one where the fellow is murdered – but before the lights went on and the curtain went up. Would that have been possible, d'you think, Dad?'

Hodgkiss thought about that then nodded his head. 'Yes. It would not have been at all difficult for someone to do that because putting the plant stand on its spot was the first thing I did during that scene change. After that I did the sideboard with some help from the fellow playing the inspector, then the sofa, the table and the chair. I used a torch to get everything set so whoever moved it would have had enough light to see what he was doing while I was making the other changes. Perhaps I should say he or she.'

'Fine,' said Esme. 'So now we know when it was moved. Now we have to figure out why. Why would someone move it just a few feet and why in that direction? That's what we have to figure out.'

'What's that odd bit of equipment on the wall back there?' said the constable pointing to the dim recesses at the back of the stage.

Esme explained: 'That's the old switchboard. That's where all the lighting for the play was operated. There were different lights used in the various scenes. Spotlights had to be set and turned on and off. It was quite a complicated business at times.'

The constable acknowledged the information with a vague nod. 'Then I don't suppose whoever did the lighting could have also had a part in the play as well, could he? I mean, did he double up as an actor by any chance. I know sometimes an actor can play two or more parts so I thought maybe this fellow who did the lighting might have doubled as an actor in some minor part.'

Esme shook her head. 'No. He only did the lights. Fellow named Fred Cahill.'

Constable Cullen looked disappointed. 'It just struck me that if for some reason he had to do a bit of acting as well as the lights he might have moved that plant stand a bit to one side to clear the way if he had to come on stage.'

Hodgkiss smiled broadly. 'You are a very bright young man, Constable Cullen. Now at last we are getting somewhere.'

'Are we?' said Esme, sceptically. 'Delighted to hear it, Dad. Now perhaps you'd like to tell us exactly where we're getting because I can't see it.'

Hodgkiss inclined his head towards where the plant stand

stood. 'Come with me and I'll show you. Or rather, the constable here will show you because Donald would certainly not permit me to do what needs to be done.'

The constable looked blankly at Hodgkiss. 'What needs to be done? What am I going to show you?'

'You are about to show us where the cunning Mr Cahill hid the knives; the fake one which was last seen apparently in the victim's chest and the real one that actually killed him. Now, Constable, will you kindly explore the contents of the jardinière on that plant stand. To do it you will need an implement of some sort so you don't leave your fingerprints where they should not be. Just wait a moment please.'

Hodgkiss detoured into the wings and returned with a short wooden ruler. 'This was on the sound effects table … heaven alone knows what sound it was supposed to simulate. A child being chastised perhaps.' He handed the ruler to Constable Cullen. 'Now, constable I want you to dig around in the sand at the bottom of that jardinière to see what you can find for us.'

The constable shrugged, took the ruler, peered into the jardinière and began to poke about in the layer of sand in the bottom.

He looked up sharply. 'You're right, Mr Hodgkiss. There's something in there all right … something buried at the bottom under the sand.' He took a thin glove from his pocket, pulled it on his right hand and reached into the jardinière.

The hand came out holding a knife with a long thin blade and a second knife, a rather clumsy, unlikely thing made of plastic.

Constable Cullen said: 'Bingo!'

*　　*　　*

'That was very clever work, Edgar,' said Superintendent O'Hare, dabbing his lips with a paper serviette.

O'Hare's ample bulk was wedged into the pine breakfast nook in the Burke's kitchen opposite Donald and Hodgkiss.

Behind them at the kitchen bench Esme was preparing to serve a dessert of hot homemade apple pie with cream to supplement the baked lamb dinner the remains of which she had just cleared away, all the plates clean to the last smear of gravy.

Donald had invited his superior officer to dinner knowing that the superintendent, a bachelor, looked forward to Esme's home-cooked dinners.

Unwilling to see his father-in-law receiving such fulsome praise from the superintendent, Donald was determined to apply a damper.

'Yeah. I guess it was pretty clever,' Donald conceded unwillingly, 'but I reckon we're still a long way from having enough evidence to be sure of getting a conviction. There's nothing to disprove that Cahill fellow's statement that he never actually moved away from his spot at the old switchboard, and we've got absolutely nothing to show that he ever set foot on the stage.'

O'Hare nodded. 'You've got a point there, Donald. It'd be great if somehow we could show that he left his post at the lighting gear at the back wall.'

Esme, who had been following the conversation, turned suddenly from the bench.

'I know how you might be able to prove he came onto the stage,' she said.

'Oh yes,' said Donald sceptically, shaking his head and rolling his eyes towards the ceiling. 'Do tell.'

Esme ignored the slight. 'Remember when I tripped over

that silly rug and dropped the decanter. Well, its stopper came out and spilled some of that sticky orange syrup on the rug. Now if Cahill had come across the stage as far as the chair where Archer was tied up the chances are he would have stepped on the rug and maybe in that puddle of syrup without knowing it. If he *did* step in it it'd certainly have messed up the soles of his shoes and that would prove that he was on stage around the right time to do the stabbing and just near where he'd have to be to actually do it.'

O'Hare's eyes flew wide. 'The woman's a genius.' He turned to Hodgkiss. 'A real chip off the old block.'

Donald winced.

O'Hare continued enthusiastically. 'All we've got to do is examine the shoes Cahill was wearing on the night and if there's sign at all of that stuff on them we'll have him. If he *did* tread in it he probably wouldn't realise it because it was dark so chances are he wouldn't have tried to scrub it off afterwards. I'd say our boys in the lab will have no trouble finding traces of it and establishing where it came from if it was that syrup.'

Esme continued. 'And it would prove that he came onto the stage about the time of the murder because I dropped that bottle only minutes before the end of the scene when the murder happened.'

'Well done, Esme,' said the superintendent accepting a plate with a large serving of pie and cream. 'You're a wonder. Donald doesn't know how lucky he is having you and Edgar around to help.'

He plunged a spoon into the pie, signed contentedly and raised a hearty serving to his mouth.

* * *

Two days later Donald came home with the news that the police laboratory had found strong traces of orange cordial on the shoes that Fred Cahill had worn during the fatal performance.

'He's spilled the beans big time,' he announced to Hodgkiss and Esme who were seated amicably together in the breakfast nook enjoying a late afternoon tea.

Donald continued, slipping into the seat beside Hodgkiss: 'He swears that he was put up to it by the mayor, Cr McCann and the fellow who wrote the play, Chester Roberts.

'He's confessed to stabbing Archer and hiding the two knives in that pot on the plant stand. He said that he had to put some extra sand in it to make sure the knives were completely covered.

'I guess that's when he spilt the sand that you noticed, Dad.

'He says it was all part of a plan worked out by the mayor and his mates to get rid of Archer so they could somehow bribe or cheat their way into owning that old theatre Archer told you about.

'He also reckoned that Victoria Anderson and McCann had got together with Chester Roberts over the script and specially wrote that scene so it would create the opportunity to kill Archer. Sounds a bit far fetched, but I guess it's possible. The whole plot was pretty whacky.'

'One thing I can't understand,' said Esme, 'is how on earth did Cahill manage to find the chair where Archer was tied up? I mean, it was pitch black on the stage and in the hall after the lights went out and Dad closed the curtains.'

Donald nodded. 'Yeah, the superintendent and I wondered about that too, so we asked Cahill. You'll never guess how he did it. He put two small dabs of phosphorescent paint on the back of the legs of the chair Archer was tied to. That way he had plenty of time to get out there, do the job and get back to the switchboard in time to turn the lights back on after the curtain was closed and the applause had died down.'

'And I suppose the sound of all the clapping would have covered any noise he happened to make,' Esme added.

Donald nodded 'Yeah. And he reckoned that he never saw you drop the decanters so he never knew about the spilled orange syrup.'

Hodgkiss frowned. 'It's a pity in many ways.'

'A pity!' Donald barked. 'How's it a pity? We've caught a nasty killer and the greedy so-and-sos who put him up to it. I thought you'd be pleased.'

'Well, of course I'm pleased, but look at it from Esme's point of view for a moment. She may never have another chance to act in a play.'

'Well, that suits me fine,' said Donald. 'I wasn't at all happy about her being in that one. A French maid indeed. Never heard such nonsense.'

'I thought she looked great,' said Hodgkiss.

Donald leaned towards Hodgkiss and whispered. 'So did I, Dad. But don't you dare tell her.'

The Miraculous Message

'Of course the fellow's illiterate … or damned near.'
Frances Field was not feeling in the least charitable towards her boss, George Mason.

Pat Strong asked. 'How long have you been working for him?'

The two were seated comfortably in the living room of Pat's up-market town house located in one of the parts of Kylerbrin which estate agents referred to as the Golden Triangle.

'Five years … or nearly,' Frances replied. 'I should have heeded the warning signs the first time I met him.'

'Warning signs?' Pat asked, sipping her tea.

'Yes. The fellow wanted to hold our job interview in his local pub. I told him I didn't go to pubs. I told him he could interview me at his office or not at all.'

'And is he illiterate … really? Surely you don't mean the man can't read and write.'

'Oh he can read and write … after a fashion. When he

writes he uses mainly capital letters and he can't read without moving his lips. I have to dictate all his letters then read them over when the typist is finished with them. He wouldn't know if half the words were incorrectly spelled, which they usually are. Even the girl who does the typing is hopeless.'

'Then why on earth do you stay there?'

'For the money of course. He pays well otherwise I'd have gone long ago.'

'So what's the problem now?' Pat asked. 'You said on the phone that you were having to leave. What's happened?'

'Well I've just discovered that in addition to being illiterate and a disgusting slob the man is also a crook.'

'A crook?' Pat echoed.

'Yes. A crook. And a dangerous one at that. There's no other way of putting it.'

'Why? What's he been up to?'

'You know I'm the company secretary and I do all the books. Well it didn't take me long to work out that lately he hasn't been doing nearly as he had been in the past year or two. Then recently, very recently, I discovered that all of a sudden business had turned around and he was making a good deal more money than previously. The whole business had been going slowly backwards for more than two years. He couldn't compete with the big pharmaceutical companies any more. Recently the big two companies had gone on a marketing drive to push up sales and of course we were the collateral damage. We both knew it. We'd actually discussed it on a number of occasions. At one meeting he asked me if I knew anyone who might come on board and give us a few marketing tips to see if sales could be improved. I gave him a few names of people I knew but he didn't contact any of them. I knew he wouldn't because of course marketing costs money.

That was more than a year ago. Then a couple of months ago I noticed that the figures had dramatically turned around. It didn't take long to find out why. He'd changed our suppliers. The people who sold him the raw materials for his herbal remedies had disappeared off the books and I discovered he was now buying most of his stuff on the cheap from a supplier with a very dodgy reputation in the trade. Half of the stuff they deliver is mixed with grass and all sorts of rubbish and some of it is even contaminated according to some of the people I've asked in the factory. I was so concerned that I sent samples of some of our pills and capsules to a chemist I know. He rang back the very next day. He sounded quite alarmed over the phone. He told me that he'd tested some of our things and he was amazed that people hadn't been seriously ill or even died. He's since sent me a written report confirming it.'

'And have you spoken to this Mason fellow about it?'

'Yes. I tackled him about it last week.'

'And what did he say?'

'He denied it of course. Not that he'd changed suppliers, he couldn't very well deny that, but he denied that the new supplier was sending us dodgy product. I told him that was nonsense and he knew it. I told him about the tests on the samples. I told him that if he continued to buy supplies from that fellow I'd have no choice but to report him to the standards people.'

'And how did he take that?'

'How do you think he took it? Not at all well. We had a bit of a shouting match and I went home.'

'So what happens now?'

'I expect he'll send me my wages in lieu of notice and that will be the end of it.'

'And will you report it … what he's selling now?'

'Oh definitely. People could get quite sick if they swallow some of his pills and potions.'

She leaned down and picked up a brief case from behind the sofa where she sat. She placed it in her lap and patted it.

'It's all in here,' she said. 'I even souvenired the company's books. They tell the whole story. The health department people would only have to go and look at the new suppliers' warehouses and test the stuff they're sending him. The suppliers would be charged under the Act and closed down and so would Mason. He could get a heavy fine and even go to gaol, particularly if anyone gets sick from taking his stuff which is really quite on the cards.'

Pat frowned. 'But do you think you should have actually taken his books away. Couldn't you have copied them?'

'What! And let him shred these. Not on your life. If I didn't have the originals he might worm his way out of it somehow. He's not above paying bribes … or so I've heard. Now he's pretty desperate, which brings me to why I'm here, Pat. Would you look after these for me for a week or two while this matter is sorted out. I believe that he's not above trying to steal them back he's so desperate.'

Pat did not like the idea of becoming involved in this unsavoury matter, but agreed nevertheless.

'All right, Frances. As it happens I have a safe. I'll put them there.'

'Thanks, Pat. That's a weight of my mind.'

*　　*　　*

'Bloody know-all bitch.'

George Mason was not happy. 'Just because she went to

university she thinks she knows the lot. Well, she's got a thing or two to learn if she reckons she can do this to me.'

Seated across George Mason's wide desk in the office of Good 4U Foods Fred Baker clucked his sympathy.

'Yeah. And she took off with the account books too. You oughta have the cops onto her for that, boss. That's theft.'

Mason said hurriedly. 'I don't think we need to involve the police at this stage, Fred.'

'Well you can't let her get away with it. After all, what's she complaining about ... we switched suppliers, that's all. What's wrong with that?'

Mason sighed. Fred was loyal, but that was about all that could be said in his favour.

There was a short silence, then Fred asked. 'So what are we going to do about it, boss? About her?'

Mason nodded thoughtfully. 'I think we've got to take steps to get those books back ASAP.'

Fred nodded agreement. 'Sure thing. So where d'you reckon she'd keep them?' Promptly Fred answered his own question. 'I guess she'd take them home. Keep them there.'

Mason pulled a face. 'Maybe. Now, what would you do, Fred, if you'd taken something that didn't belong to you and you thought the owner might take steps to get them back again?'

Fred thought. 'I'd hide them. That's what I'd do.' 'At home? Would you hide them at home?'

Fred thought again. 'Maybe not. I'd hide them somewhere else.'

Mason nodded. 'Exactly. So would I. But where?'

'Maybe I'd ask a friend to look after them for me.'

'OK. Now do we know any of Mrs Field's friends? People she might get to hide things for her."

Fred shook his head gloomily. 'Can't say I do, off-hand.'

'No. Nor do I,' said Mason. 'So there's not a lot we can do, although I suppose it wouldn't do any harm to take a look around her place just in case she's left them lying around somewhere.'

'You want me to do that ... take a look around her place?'

'If you wouldn't mind, Fred.'

'No problem, boss. When? When do you want me to do it?'

'When you know she's not there. Her husband goes to work in town every day so he shouldn't be a problem. I think the thing to do is for me to ask her to come and meet me somewhere to talk the whole thing over then you can have a look around without any interruptions.'

'So when will you have this meeting?'

'I'll give her a ring tomorrow maybe and see what I can arrange. She should be prepared to meet me just to talk things over. I could make out that I'd be prepared to go along with whatever she wants.'

'Then you'll get her to come over here?'

Mason thought about that. 'Maybe not. Maybe it'd be best to meet her at your place, Fred, if that's OK with you?'

'It's fine with me, boss,' Fred said hurriedly. 'Any time.'

'Fred's Place' was, of course, strictly speaking, not Fred's Place at all. It was the home, until very recently, owned and occupied by George Mason's father, Robert. Robert had shuffled off his mortal coil less than a month previously, leaving all his worldly goods to George and his elder brother Alfred, who was living and working in London.

Alfred had returned briefly to Sydney for their father's funeral and, before returning to London, had instructed his younger brother to prepare the house for sale, get the best price he could for it, then send Alfred his half of the proceeds.

Because the house was still full of the late Robert's worldly goods the brothers had agreed that it would be desirable to have the house occupied until it was sold, as a deterrent to burglars.

Thus Fred Baker found himself living in a very well furnished, desirable bungalow, rent free.

A feature of the home was a large cellar and since Robert had been something of a wine connoisseur the cellar was stocked with a large quantity of vintage wine accommodated in tall, double-sided custom-made racks. This wine, Robert had impressed upon both his sons, was already valuable and getting more valuable with each passing year.

Since neither son was fond of wine – Alfred favoured whisky and George was definitely a beer man – the wine was to be the subject of a separate sale before the house was auctioned.

'I'll ring her now,' said George, taking the mobile phone from his shirt pocket. 'I'll suggest she bring the book with her.'

Frances took the call with some surprise and agreed, rather unwillingly, to meet the following day at the home of the late Robert Mason. She declined utterly to bring the company's books.

'What do you think, George,' she asked, 'that I came down in the last shower?'

'I just thought we might be able to reach some agreement over this business.'

'Do you seriously think I'll ever go along with the sort of dangerous scam you're involved in.'

'Dangerous! How's it dangerous?' George demanded. 'I've just switched suppliers to someone who doesn't charge the earth.'

Frances Field snorted. 'Well you're already charging your customers for the earth because according to my information dirt makes up quite a large percentage of the goods you've been selling.'

'That's nonsense,' George protested. 'What makes you think that?'

'I think that because that's what the report from my chemist friend told me. Would you like to know what else he had to say?'

'No. But I suppose I'm going to hear it anyway, aren't I.'

'You should be glad to. According to him some of your things are so toxic that it's lucky some of your customers haven't fallen seriously ill or died.'

'Oh that's nonsense,' said George. 'He's exaggerating.'

'I don't think so. I'd be happy to bring you a copy of his report and I can assure you he knows what he's talking about.'

'Well you had no right to send him any of my products for analysis without my approval.'

'You should be thankful that I did. Anyway, what do you expect this meeting to achieve?'

'I think that somehow you've got the wrong end of the stick about this whole business. You seem to think that I've deliberately been doing something crook. Nothing could be further from the truth. In fact …'

'Enough, George. Hold it for the meeting, but I warn you I'll take a lot of convincing that what you did in switching suppliers was anything less than an attempt to cut costs and save money.'

'And what's wrong with that? The big boys were making things really tough for us. You know that better than anyone.'

'Yes, I couldn't argue with that, but …'

'Then what's the problem?'

'How many times do I have to say it. The stuff you're sending out to the shops is bad, nasty, it's damned dangerous. I'll show you the reports.'

'OK. Until tomorrow.'

He cut the connection. He turned to Fred. 'Tomorrow arvo. You can have a look around her place in case she's left my books lying around. You know where she lives, right?'

Fred nodded.

*　　*　　*

'Of course she was never the easiest person to get along with.'

Clad in her two-piece swimsuit Pat Strong was stretched out on the plastic sun lounge on the north-facing balcony off her upstairs bedroom.

She added. 'Frances always had to be in the right. And I suppose she usually was.'

Seated in a shady corner of the balcony Edgar Hodgkiss remarked. 'Those sorts of people can be a little hard to take at times. So what do you think? Is she really onto something?'

'Oh definitely,' Pat said quickly. 'If Frances says something funny is going on in that company you can bet that it is. Particularly as she did the books for them. No one would be better placed than her to pick up on some dodgy activities.'

'So what does she say this fellow's been up to?'

'Apparently she noticed that they were suddenly making money after he'd been in the red for a long time. She did some checking and found that the turn-around came at the same time as they changed suppliers.'

'Suppliers?'

'Yes. The people they get their raw material from … the

stuff they use to make their herbal remedies … pills, capsules, powders … you know.'

'So now they're getting the stuff on the cheap.'

'Yes, but Frances said it's not only cheap. It's cheap and nasty.'

'And has she raised the matter with her boss?'

'Oh yes. That's when the trouble started. Of course he denied that there was anything untoward going on. So she took the company's books away with her and she's planning to take the whole thing to the appropriate government authority … whoever that is. She's also had the stuff tested by an independent chemist who's confirmed that it's pretty inferior. In fact according to this chemist he's surprised that it hasn't been making people sick.'

Just then the mobile phone on the balcony deck beside where Pat lay sounded its ringtone.

She scooped up the phone and opened the connection.

'Yes, Bernard. We were just talking about her. Edgar and I. You know Edgar, don't you? Yes.'

There was a short silence while Pat listened. From where he sat Hodgkiss could hear the faint buzz of an agitated male voice.

'That's rather disturbing,' said Pat. 'Particularly in view of the circumstances.'

The buzzing voice continued urgently.

'Well, Bernard, I don't see quite what we can do at the moment. I mean, you're not even sure where she went, are you? Why don't you just wait a little while. She'll probably come home and tell you all about it. Yes. Yes. Keep in touch.'

Pat cut the connection and replaced the phone on the deck.

'That was Bernard Field, Fran's husband.'

'He sounded as if he was in a bit of a state,' Hodgkiss observed.

'Yes, he is. He just arrived home and Fran wasn't there. He's got into a tizzy because she didn't leave a note. Apparently Fran always leaves a note if she's going out unexpectedly. And of course now he thinks that she's gone off to meet her boss to have a confrontation over this business.'

'Oh for heaven's sake,' said Hodgkiss. 'What a panic merchant.'

'Yes, he is rather,' said Pat. 'But if she *has* gone off to meet this fellow ...'

'Yes, what were you going to say?'

'Just that it might not have been very wise to have gone alone, that's all.'

'And what makes you say that. Does he have a history of violence?'

'No. Fran said nothing about that. Just that I suppose he might be rather desperate if he thinks she's going to make real trouble for him ... as she could, that is if her information about his pills and things is right, and she seemed pretty sure of herself. Anyway, Bernard's going to ring me when she comes home and tell me what happened.'

*   *   *

Frances Field was furious.

How dare that ghastly man lock her in this place ... a wine cellar, full of rows and rows of racks full of bottles of wine.

She should have anticipated that George might resort to something like this when she turned up without the books.

But surely he realised that now he could get into much bigger trouble, virtually kidnapping her, than she could make for him by reporting his dangerous herbs to the authorities.

She had arrived at the address at precisely two as arranged.

He'd said something about it being where his father lived. She remembered him coming to the office one morning a month or so ago and telling her that his father had died and that he would be away from the office for a few days because his brother was arriving from England for the funeral and then, of course, there would be other arrangement to be made. She had not seen him for three days, then he had come back and it had been business as usual, although she knew that he was having discussions with some estate agent over sale of the house. And there were plans, too, for some wine to be sent to an auction house that specialised in wine sales.

When she arrived she had been met at the door by a very large man who had not given his name and made her wait on the doorstep while he fetched George.

As soon as they were settled in the living room George had asked if she had brought the company books with her and she told him no, then reminded him that she had already told him that on the phone when they arranged the meeting.

He had seemed to shrug that off and began to quiz her about the report from the chemist that she had mentioned.

She had taken the pages from her deep carry bag and given them to him. She had watched as he read them, his face falling as he turned the pages over on the desk where he sat.

When he had finished he had stacked the pages neatly together then handed them back to her.

'It's all nonsense of course, Frances,' he had said, then added, 'but even so it could be very damaging for the company if any of this stuff leaked out.'

She had laughed. 'It's not going to leak out, George,' she had told him. 'I'll be handing it straight to the pure foods people. You don't seriously think that I'm about to stand by and do nothing while you continue to sell stuff to the public that can actually cause harm ... even death.'

He had shaken his head, smiling ruefully. 'You can't seriously believe that, Fran,' he had said. 'The fellow who wrote that stuff didn't know what he was talking about. Of course, there's a certain amount of dirt in the herbs when they're delivered to the store rooms. But it's all taken out in the cleaning process.'

'That's the trouble: it's not. My fellow found dirt in the capsules and worse, insect parts, spider legs. How would you explain that?'

'I don't have to explain it,' he had snapped. 'It's nonsense. Why, I wouldn't be surprised if you'd pay him to say it to help trump up a case against me?'

She had laughed. 'And why would I want to trump up a case against you. I'll have to find another job now, and I must say you did pay well for my services.'

They had continued to argue but it had gone nowhere. George would not accept that her chemist's report was accurate and she had no doubt it was.

Then he had lost his temper. She had never seen him in such a state before. He had leapt up from where he had been reading the report at an old rolltop desk and had crossed the room to where she was sitting.

'Don't think you can hold me to ransom like this, Frances. You've taken on the wrong person if you think you can blackmail me.'

She had tried to remain calm although now she felt physically threatened.

'I am not trying to blackmail you, George,' she had said quietly. 'I'm trying to make you see that ...'

But he had cut her off. 'Of course you are,' he had blustered.

'Just say how much … how much money do you want to go away and take this ridiculous lying report with you. Five thousand … ten thousand … twenty thousand. How much?'

His eyes were bulging and spit showered down from his mouth as he shouted at her.

'How much?'

'I'm not interested in your money, George,' she had said. 'You don't understand, you really don't. All I want is for you to stop selling things to the public that can do harm. That's all I want.'

'So if I stop selling for now, then you'll forget about this,' he had said, holding up the report.

'If you stop selling contaminated product I'll forget about it,' she had conceded.

'And you won't show this report to anyone?'

She had agreed to that, unwillingly.

He had turned away then quickly back again.

He reached out and seized her right arm just below the shoulder.

'Frances, I don't believe you. I don't trust you. I know if I let you go with this report you'll be straight off to the health department and have me closed down. That's what you'll do, isn't it?'

When she had not replied he had dragged her to her feet.

She had protested. 'Stop it, George, you're hurting me. Let me go.'

But he had not let her go. Instead he had dragged her out of the room into the hall. Along the hall he had opened a door leading down to a cellar. He had literally pushed her down the steep wooden stairs and she had saved herself from a nasty fall by holding onto a wooden rail attached to the wall.

She had cried out but her cries had echoed around the cellar.

He had left her there, locking the heavy wooden door behind him.

She had lost no time in exploring the cellar for some way out, but there was none. There was not even a window she could see out.

Luckily there was electric light turned on by a switch on the wall just inside the door at the top of the steps, so she would not have to stay there in the dark, assuming that he left her there any length of time.

She glanced at her watch. It was only four o'clock, slightly more than two hours since she had arrived at this place.

She realised with a shock that her handbag containing her phone was still in the room upstairs where she had confronted the man.

She shook her head in dismay. She thought: how long does the silly man think he can keep me here.

*   *   *

Upstairs George Mason and Frank Baker were considering the same question.

'Jees, you can't keep her here for ever, boss,' said Frank.

'I'm not planning to keep her forever, Frank, but I *am* going to keep her here for just as long as it takes. Do you have a problem with that?'

'Nah, of course I don't. It's just that if we keep her here someone, her husband probably, will decide to go to the cops then we'll have people out everywhere looking for her.'

George nodded thoughtfully. 'Yeah. Maybe you're right. But who's going to come *here* looking for her. No one knows about you living here, do they? An she doesn't know you work for me because you're always out at the storage area so the two of you have never run across each other. So the cops won't have any reason to look here, Right?'

Frank gave the matter careful thought then nodded. 'S'right.'

'But you're right just the same, Frank. It'd be best if no one started to worry about her just yet, or start wondering where she might be. So how about this; you've got her bag there with her phone in it. Why don't you take it downstairs, give her the phone and tell her to send a message to her husband letting him know that everything's cool, that she's taken time out to think things over and she'll be home soon.'

'You want me to give her the phone back?' Frank asked, anxiously. 'D'you think that's a good idea, boss.'

'It'll be OK if you're there to keep an eye on her. Tell her she can send her husband a text message. She can write it but it doesn't go until I say it's OK. Tell her if she tries anything smart she'll have cause to regret it.'

'OK, boss. Let me get this straight; I give her the phone back and I tell her she's to send a text to her husband saying that she's OK, that everything's fine, but she's not to send it til' I've checked it over with you. Right?'

'One hundred per cent.'

'And you want me to do it now?'

George smiled, shaking his head. Oh no. No. Not yet. Let's give her some time to think things over down there in the cellar. Time to work out that we're fair dinkum. Meanwhile, get her something to eat later on … maybe a hamburger and a coffee from down the road … and maybe tomorrow she can do the text. Right? Have you got her phone there?'

'It's here in the bag,' said Frank picking up the bag, reaching in and coming out with a small mobile phone.

*　　*　　*

In the cellar Frances Field was still fuming.

How long did those morons think they could keep her locked up here? And who was that big gorilla who opened the door to her. She'd never seen him around the office.

When she grew tired of speculating she decided to make a closer inspection of her surroundings. She was fond of a glass of wine with a meal, red wine in particular, and the cellar seemed to be devoted to red wines exclusively. As she went from rack to rack examining the bottles her admiration grew for whoever it was who had put together this collection of vintages. Some of these bottles, she knew from browsing in bottle shops, were worth large sums of money. Maybe I'll crack a bottle later she thought, that is if they think to feed me.

She glanced at her watch. Going on seven. It must be getting dark outside, she thought. Dinner time.

The thought had no sooner occurred to her when she heard a key in the lock of the door. She hurried back towards the stairs in time to see the man who had let her into the house open the door and set down a tray on the top step.

'Dinner,' he announced. 'Hope you like hamburgers.'

'Never mind the hamburgers,' Frances called as she hurried up the steps. 'How much longer do you think you can keep me here? You realise my husband will have contacted the police by now and reported me missing. They'll be looking for me.'

'But they won't look here, will they?' said the man, smiling unpleasantly.

Frances made a dash for the door but the man moved quickly in front of her, placing both hands on her shoulders.

'Take it easy, lady. You're not going anywhere until the boss says so.'

'And when will the boss say so?' she asked, her voice trembling with rage.

'When you decide to co-operate, not before.'

The man retreated, closed the door firmly and Frances heard the lock turn.

She picked up the tray and carried it down the stairs. She sat on the bottom step and unwrapped the hamburger.

She thought. 'Well, red wine for meat. Let's see what we can find that might be drinkable.'

Frances crossed to the nearest rack of wines and began a systematic inspection of the contents. At last she settled on a bottle of shiraz and returned to the step and sat.

She drank the coffee down and tipped the plastic mug upside down to drain.

Since the wine she had selected was bottled before the advent of the screw top, she stood and brought the neck down heavily on one of the higher steps. The neck broke neatly and some of the wine spilled onto the step.

She inspected the neck, satisfied that it was a clean break, then began to pour wine cautiously into the empty mug, straining it through a cotton handkerchief.

She settled down once more on the bottom step and undid the hamburger.

'A meal I will remember for some time to come,' she thought.

When the hamburger and the wine were gone she climbed the steps and struck her fist firmly on the door. She called: 'Hello, is there anybody there. George, are you there?'

There was a short silence then she heard footsteps approaching.

'What do you want, lady?' No doubt it was that rather uncouth fellow who had let her in and fed her.

'Are you planning to keep me locked in here all night?' she asked.

'Looks like it,' said the man.

'And where, pray, do you expect me to sleep? On the floor?'

After a short silence the man replied: 'If you look in the far corner on your right you'll find some old wine cartons. You could sleep on them. They'll keep you warm too if you pull them up over you. Better than newspapers, or so I'm told.'

'Oh thank you so much,' she replied, laying on the sarcasm. 'I suppose it would be too much to ask for a pillow.'

'Sweet dreams,' said the man, and footsteps retreated.

'Bastard,' she said under her breath and returned down the stairs to explore the distant corner of the cellar in search of the wine cartons.

*   *   *

When Frances woke the next morning she did not at once take in her strange surroundings. Memory was not assisted by the amount of red wine she had consumed hours earlier in her difficult quest for sleep.

She threw off the cardboard covering that had kept her body warm during the night and rose painfully to her feet. She had left the lights on all night and now she made her way to the stairs and up to the door. Once there she tried the handle in the faint hope that her captor may have relented and left the door unlocked.

Disappointed she began to beat vigourously on the thick wooden panels with her fists.

Soon she heard approaching footsteps. There was the sound of the key turning in the lock and the door was pulled back.

The man stood there. 'Sleep well?' he asked.

'Don't be ridiculous. How could I sleep? I don't suppose I'm going to be fed, am I?'

'Yes of course you are, but the boss wants you to do something for him first.'

'Oh and what's that?' she asked suspiciously. 'If he thinks I'm going to hand back those books …;

But the man held up a huge hand. 'Nothing like that. He just wants you to send a text message to your husband saying how well you're being treated and not to worry and you'll be home again soon.'

She asked. 'And is that true? Will I be going home soon?'

'That's what the boss says.'

'And that makes it right, does it?'

'It does so far as I'm concerned.' The man reached into his pocket and took out her mobile phone. He held it out to her but when her hand closed on it she found it remained in the man's grip.

'Not so fast,' he said. 'When you've finished writing your message don't send it. Just give the phone back to me. I'll ring the boss on my phone and read the message over to him. If he says it's OK I'll send the message for you. OK. Now take the phone, but remember this; I'll be watching what you write and if you send the message before the boss has cleared it you will be down here for a long, long time and you mightn't get fed very often. Understood?'

Frances nodded. 'Understood,' she repeated.

The man released the phone into Frances' hand and she took it back down the stairs the man hard on her heels.

Frances and sat on the bottom step, thinking, the man lowered himself to sit cosily beside her.

The man said. 'Well get on with it. The sooner it's done

the sooner I can send it off and you can settle down for the night.'

Frances began pecking out letters on the tiny keypad, pausing now and then to think before continuing.

The man leaned over her shoulder, eyes on the screen.

It was only a matter of minutes before Frances handed over the phone.

'There you are. I think George should agree to that. I've been careful not to mention where I am and I've said I'm being treated well and not to worry. Is that what he wants?'

The man shrugged. 'Sounds fine to me,' he said, scrambling to his feet and heading back up the stairs. 'I'll have to read it over to him. I'll let you know if he says it's fine and that I've sent it.'

'Thank you, I'd appreciate that,' she said as he closed and locked the door again.

As he carried the phone through to the kitchen, where his own phone was charging on a work bench, Fred read the message.

> I'm with Mr Mason working on a new project. Its OK so
> don't you worry or I'll worry to. Sorry. I should of made
> some dinners for you before I left so go out to a hotel. If
> you still have the flue take some milk and honey To Ward
> it of. Don't worry. Their treating me fine. Love Fran.

Fred decided that the message seemed innocuous enough so he picked up his phone and thumbed the key pad.

'She's written the message, boss,' he announced. 'Seems OK to me.'

'Does it indeed,' said George Mason testily. 'Well, I think I'll decide whether it's OK or not. You never know what kind of tricks a smart-alec bitch like her might try. Just read it over, will you, Fred.'

Fred read over the email. 'That's the lot,' he said. 'Harmless enough don't you think.'

'I suppose so,' said George. 'That's all she put, is it?'

'Every last word. Will I send it?'

'Yes, send it but hang on to the phone. I might want her to send more messages some time to keep her husband quiet.'

'She wanted to know when we're letting her go. Can I tell her something?'

'Yes, Fred. You can tell her that she's going to be there until I'm satisfied that she's not going to try to put me out of business when I let her out. Tell her that.'

'OK,' said Fred, cutting the connection.

He thumbed the send button on the keypad then walked back to the cellar door and knocked.

Moments later the woman's voice came. 'Did he say to send the message?'

'Oh yeah. The message was fine. I've sent it. But Mr Mason said to tell you that you're going to stay there until he's sure that you won't make trouble for him when he lets you out.'

The woman nearly screamed. 'Not make trouble! What! He thinks he can hold me prisoner in his rotten cellar as long as he likes. What fantasy world does he live in?'

Fred heard the woman stamping away down the stairs.

*   *   *

The next night, try as she did, sleep did not come to Frances.

She tried re-arranging her cardboard bedclothes, twisting from one side to the other. At last she gave up and lay, thinking.

She had no doubt that her email would have puzzled and worried Bernard but she doubted if he would have been able to winkle out from the text the address of the house where she was being held.

The more she thought about her situation the angrier she became. After all, Mason was nothing but a crook who was placing the health of the community in danger by selling contaminated goods.

He had to be stopped and she was the only person who could stop him because she was the only one who knew what he was doing.

But what could she do, locked up here in this damned wine cellar. A very expensive wine cellar at that.

Then it struck her. If Mason could hold her hostage she could hold Mason's valuable wine hostage.

She threw back her cardboard covers and hurried through the cellar, up the stairs. At the top of the stairs she paused to look at her watch. It was just before one a.m.

She began thumping on the door and calling out.

It was more than five minutes before she heard footsteps approaching with a measured tread.

'What the hell are you on about now? Do you know what time it is?'

Yes, it's nearly one in the morning. Now, listen carefully, I want you to ring Mr Mason with an important message.'

'Ring him at this hour! No way, lady. I'll ring him in the morning.'

'No, Mr Whoever-You-Are, you'll ring him now, because in five minutes I will begin smashing the bottles of wine down here and I won't stop until every last one is broken. Have you got that?'

'If you did that he'd kill you. They're very valuable. He had them seen by an expert. Besides, they don't belong just to him. His father left them to him and his brother.'

'Then his brother won't be pleased, will he. So just ring him with the message.'

'No way, lady. I'll ring him in the morning.'

'Then just wait a minute, will you,' she called. 'Don't go yet. Stay where you are.'

She turned and hurried down the steps and stood before the nearest wine rack. It was an impressive structure, taller than her five foot nine inches.

She leaned against it but it wouldn't budge. She stepped back, put her hands against two wooden uprights and pushed with all her weight. But it rocked only slightly then righted again.

She stepped back and ran at it, hitting a row of bottles with her shoulder.

The thing teetered and slowly fell backwards with a satisfying crash accompanied by the sound of breaking bottles.

The man's voice came urgently through the door. 'What the hell are you up to?'

She screamed in return. 'That's the first one. The next one will go over in three minutes unless you ring now. Tell him I'll smash the lot unless I'm out of here in five minutes.'

'OK I'll ring him. Just wait. OK?'

'You've got three minutes before the next one goes over,' she called in reply.

She stood at the bottom of the steps waiting, eyes on her watch.

When the three minutes had passed she walked around to confront the next wine rack. She took three paces back, lowered her head and charged with her shoulder.

Again the rack shuddered then crashed over.

At once a voice came from the door at the top of the stairs. 'Hey, that wasn't three minutes.'

'It was by my watch. Have you rung Mason?'

'Yeah. I rang him. He wasn't pleased.'

'I didn't think he would be. Is he going to let me out now?'

'No. He said I was to stop you doing any more damage down there.'

'Well, good luck. Because here goes another one.'

She stepped back and charged at another of the racks with the same result.

Red wine was now making large puddles on the concrete floor.

The door flew open and the large man hurried down the stairs. 'OK. The fun's over. No more of that. That stuffs very expensive.'

'I know that' said Frances, 'That's why I'm doing it. And if you want me to stop you'll have to make me.'

She flung herself at another of the racks which went the same way as the others.

She turned, prepared to make a run at another rack when the man seized her around the waist.

She swung a fist at him, making contact with an ear. 'Take your hands off me, you great oaf.'

To underline the seriousness of her intention she dug the nails of her right hand into his left cheek and dragged her hand down, leaving a row of bloody furrow.

The man screamed. 'You bloody bitch.'

He seized her by the throat to restrain her.

As a method of restraint it was ineffective because her hands remained free. With one hand she took a bottle of old burgundy from a nearby rack and swung it heavily on to the crown of her captor's head.

Immediately he released her and nursed his head with both hands.

Finding herself at liberty Frances made a dash for the stairs only to slip in a pool of red wine.

Meanwhile the man had recovered and again seized her by both arms and dragged her away towards the back of the cellar.

'Are you going to stay with me here all day, are you?' she asked, 'because the minute you leave I'll push the rest of them over.'

Then to suit actions to her words she wriggled free and shoulder-charged the nearest rack which went over, taking another as it went.

'You gotta stop doing that,' the man said making a grab for her.

His hands closed on her throat and Frances, finding her hands still free, raked her nails once more across the man's face.

He screamed again but this time he did not let go. In fact he applied more and more pressure until he found he was virtually holding the woman up.

Only when she was no longer struggling did he release her and was rather surprised when she fell heavily to the floor and lay there.

He stooped to see what ailed her and it was some minutes before it dawned on him that she was dead.

In terror he ran up the stairs to his phone.

*　*　*

Hodgkiss was about to take his dog, Rupert, an animal of uncertain breed, to the park for his morning exercise when his mobile phone rang.

Peeved at someone ringing at such an early hour Hodgkiss

picked up the instrument with a grunt and glanced at the screen.

He thumbed open the connection. 'I was just about to take Rupert for his walk, Pat. What's happened?' he asked shortly.

'Bernard just rang. He said he's had a text from Frances and he's going to forward it to me. I'll send it on to you when I have it. OK.'

'Is that all. Then I shall look forward to seeing it,' said Hodgkiss cutting the connection abruptly as he stepped out onto the back deck to attach the harness and lead to the little dog who was waiting eagerly outside the heavy sliding door from the family room.

He had just arrived at the park and released Rupert to join his regular playmates when his phone whistled to announce the arrival of a message.

Hodgkiss called up the text and read it with mounting concern.

He thumbed his phone and called up Pat's number. 'I've read it. It's very worrying, to say the least.'

Pat agreed. 'Yes, it's so unlike her. She's always such an articulate person both in speech and writing. I've known her a long time and there was something very stilted, even phony about that message.'

'Not to mention all the grammatical errors which surely must have been deliberate. I would say that woman is in dire trouble, wouldn't you agree?'

'Yes, Edgar. Most definitely. I'm very concerned. I've tried to contact Bernard but his phone's turned off. I'll keep trying.

It was just after eight o'clock when Pat rang again. By then Hodgkiss had returned from the park and was showered and breakfasted.

'I've heard from Bernard again,' she said. 'Apparently he

had another email from Frances asking him to meet her at a particular place … he didn't say where, he just said he was going to meet her there at nine o'clock. It was all very hush-hush and mysterious. He said he would get home as soon as he could and that he would leave the back door open if we wanted to come earlier. So if you want to come with me and find out what's been going on I'll pick you up in ten minutes. Is that OK?'

'I suppose so. The whole thing is quite alarming, particularly in view of that text message. She must be in some kind of trouble to have written stuff like that. I'll be waiting outside.'

He added. 'I have a very bad feeling about this.'

Ten minutes later Hodgkiss was standing on the nature strip outside the Burke's home in a backstreet of Lillimoor when Pat's top-of-the-range Mercedes slid to the kerb.

He climbed in, attached the seat belt, and remarked: 'I've never seen so many grammatical errors in the one short message.'

Pat nodded as she pulled the car away from the kerb. 'No. It was so unlike her that it had to be contrived.'

'Well, I suppose Bernard will have picked her up and taken her home by now so we'll soon know what it was all about.'

But when they arrived at the large bungalow where the Fields lived they soon discovered that there was no one at home.

'Well, Bernard said he'd leave the back door open so let's wait inside,' said Pat.

The back door was unlocked but when they pushed it open the two stood on the threshold staring in amazement at the turmoil that greeted them in the kitchen.

The rest of the house was in a similar condition; drawers pulled open and the contents spread on the carpet, furniture pulled out of position, cushions slashed.

Hodgkiss commented. 'Obviously Bernard was lured away so the premises could be searched, wouldn't you say?'

Pat nodded. 'Searched for the account books Frances brought home from that place where she works … worked.'

'Very likely.'

'And of course they wouldn't have found them because I have them at my place.'

'You don't suppose they'll try the same stunt at your unit, do you?' Hodgkiss asked, alarmed.

Pat shook her head. 'No way, Edgar. 'It's most unlikely they'd know of Frances connection with me. We met at uni and we've hardly been bosom buddies since then. The occasional lunch together, that's all.'

'Well, let's have a look around as see if there's anything here that'll give us a clue as to where Bernard might have gone. I would say it is apparent from this that there never was a meeting with Frances.'

They'd been searching for about ten minutes before Hodgkiss, who had been examining items on a rolltop desk in the study at the front of the house, called out: 'Pat. In here. I think I might have found something.'

Moments later Pat joined him. 'What is it, Edgar. What have you found?'

Hodgkiss pointed to a blue-jacketed volume in a plastic cover with the title *Sydney Street Directory* sitting on the desk. 'First of all there's that.'

'An old Street directory?' said Pat. 'Not much use if we don't know where to look.'

Hodgkiss continued. 'Then there's that,' he said pointing to a scrap of paper sitting on the desk beside the street directory.

On the paper was written F26.

Pat nodded. 'No doubt those are the map co-ordinates for

a particular street. But it's not much use if we don't know the name of the street or which of the hundreds of street maps in the book to look for.'

Hodgkiss shook his head and smiled smugly. 'Ah, but we *do* know the name of the street.'

Pat looked at his in astonishment. 'Really?! Perhaps *you* do but I certainly don't. So what's the name of the street?'

'It was all in Frances' email. I thought you'd have worked it out by now. Do you have your phone?'

'Yes, Hodgkiss. I have my phone. No doubt you want me to call up that text so you can demonstrate how much cleverer you are than me.'

Hodgkiss nodded. 'Something like that.'

Pat took the phone from a pocket, thumbed the keypad and put it down on the desk. 'There you are, Hodgkiss. Frances' message. Now, show me where she gives the name of the street, or any street.'

'No problem,' said Hodgkiss. He dabbed his finger at the screen. 'Why do you think she used capitals there and there? Capital letters are used to denote proper nouns … correct?'

Pat frowned, then of a sudden her face broke into a beaming smile. 'Clever old Hodgkiss. Yes, I believe you're right. But there's one way to make sure.'

'Oh, and what's that?'

'Simple. If a street with that name is listed in the directory and it has beside it the same co-ordinates as those on the piece of paper, we'll know we're on the right track and we'll know where to go.'

Pat opened the street directory and thumbed through the section where street names were listed alphabetically. She paused, then with a finger followed down a column of names.

'Yes. Here it is,' she said. 'Our street, or rather *your* street, with the co-ordinates F26 beside it.'

'Then we'd better see where it is and go there, hadn't we?' said Hodgkiss.

Pat nodded, scooping up the street directory and heading for the door. 'I know where it is. It's only a few minutes away.'

Pat drove, Hodgkiss beside her, the street directory open in his lap. They had not gone far when he pointed through the windscreen. 'It's the second street on the right.'

Pat nodded. 'Fine. But what's that happening up ahead there?'

Two police cars and an ambulance were parked beside the road, their red and blue lights flashing.

Pat slowed as they approached.

'Isn't that Donald?' she asked, pointing.

Hodgkiss nodded. 'Yes, it is. I wonder what he's doing here.'

'And there's Bernard standing next to him.'

'Yes and he appears to be in handcuffs,' said Hodgkiss. 'You'd better pull over.'

Pat braked and as soon as the car had stopped Hodgkiss climbed out and began to walk quickly back to where Donald stood, hands aggressively on hips, watching his father-in-law approach.

'And what on earth are you doing here, Dad?' Donald demanded. 'And please don't say you just happened to be passing by.'

'No, Donald, I won't pretend anything of the sort. But first of all can you explain why Mr Field is in handcuffs. I'm sure there can be no justification for that.'

'Is that so,' said Donald. 'Then perhaps you can explain how he happened to be standing beside his wife's strangled body when some passers-by came along and detained him 'til I got here.'

'Really, Donald, I have no idea of Mr Field's movements this morning, however, I am confident any explanation he has given you is very likely true.'

'Oh, do you think so, do you. And do you know what kind of totally incredible explanation Mr Field gave for being here.'

'No, of course I don't.'

'Then why say there could be no justification for us holding him?'

Hodgkiss turned to Pat who had followed from the car. 'There's no point in bandying words with Donald. I think we should continue our journey.'

Pat objected. 'But what'd be the point of that. We thought that's where we'd find Bernard. Now we've found him.'

Hodgkiss nodded. 'I realise that, Pat. But that is the address where Mrs Field was held and no doubt where she was murdered.'

Pat asked anxiously. 'Then do you think it would be a good idea for the two of us to go there alone?'

'Well I can't imagine that Donald would take the least bit of interest in anything we may tell him.'

'Interest in what? Donald demanded. 'And what's this about an address where Mrs Field was murdered. What do you know, Dad, or think you know?'

Hodgkiss took a scrap of paper and pencil from his shirt pocket, wrote on it and handed it to Donald. 'Pat and I are going to that address. It is very close by. It is there we expect to find the person or persons responsible for this crime. I would prefer that you came with us for obvious reasons, but I'm quite confident that you will decide not to do so. Therefore we are obliged to deal with the matter alone.'

He turned and headed back towards the car, signaling for Pat to follow. They were half way back to the car when Hodgkiss paused.

'What is it, Edgar? Pat asked.

'Something just occurred to me. You know the old saying about criminals returning to the scene of their crime and arsonists turning out to watch their fires.'

'Yes. But I doubt if it's often true.'

'Possibly not. Nevertheless it might be worth a try. Do you have Frances' phone number with you?'

'It'll be in my phone's memory. Why?'

'I'd like to go back there and ring the number.'

Pat nodded. 'I see what you're thinking. OK. We'll give it a try.'

As they walked slowly back Pat called up Frances' number from one of the phone's menus and poised her finger over the send key.

As they approached she pressed.

Seconds passed then somewhere in the small crowd of bystanders a mobile phone played its ringtone. Immediately a large man wearing a hooded top standing in the front of the crowd, hastily took a phone from his pocket, thumbed the keypad and the ringing stopped.

'That's our man,' said Hodgkiss.

'So what do we do now?' Pat asked.

'Why, follow him of course. If he's been staying at that address he'll probably be on foot.'

They were just about to cross the road in pursuit of the man with the phone when Donald intercepted them.

'And where do you two think you're going,' he demanded.

'We have given you the address where you will find us, Donald. May I suggest you finish your work here without delay and join us there as soon as possible.'

'And what makes you think that someone at this address is responsible for that woman's death rather than her husband who was discovered leaning over her body.'

'Because that someone had Mrs Field's phone in his pocket.'

'Oh. And how do you know that?'

'Because Pat rang it and he took it out and turned it off. Then he immediately left the scene and no doubt has hurried home to inform Mason of this development. Now, may I suggest you finish what you are doing here then come to the address I have given you.'

'No way, Dad. If you reckon the person who killed her lives there then I'm coming with you.'

Pat said. 'Thank goodness for that.'

'Now, where is this place?' Donald asked.

'I'd say it is just across the road and around the corner,' said Pat.

*　　*　　*

When the three arrived at the house which Hodgkiss pointed out there was no response to Donald's repeated assaults on the brass knocker on the front door.

Giving up on a frontal attack they walked down a driveway at the side of the house and, through a bathroom window, they saw a large man using a bloodied towel to bathe angry lacerations on his face.

Donald caught the man's eye and made pointing motions to indicate that he should come to the front door.

'I know why you've come,' said the man when he opened the door.

Donald ignored the remark and asked: 'Is Mr Mason at home.'

The man shook his head. 'No. Mr Mason … he doesn't live here. He owns the place but he lets me live here.'

'And you are …?'

'Fred Baker. I work for Mr Mason.'

Donald introduced himself and displayed briefly his identity card. He didn't bother with any further introductions although Fred looked curiously at Hodgkiss and Pat.

'May we come in?' Donald inquired politely. 'There are one or two questions I need to ask you … and Mr Mason.'

The three followed Baker who led the way to a sitting room to the left off the hall.

When they were settled Donald asked: 'What can you tell us about the death of Mrs Frances Field, the lady who was found this morning in the park at the end of this street.'

'I didn' mean to kill her,' Fred said earnestly. 'I was just defending meself. Look what she did to me face?'

He turned in profile so Donald had a good view of the swollen, angry parallel scratch marks adorning his left cheek.

'And she done that too, with a wine bottle. A full one'

Fred bowed forward to display a bloody contusion on the top of his head.

He added. 'It was self-defence. No jury would convict me after what she done to me.'

'Well, let's leave that to the jury, will we, Mr Baker,' said Donald. 'Now, can you tell me why Mrs Field was here?'

'Mr Mason wanted me to keep her here?'

'He wanted you to keep her here,' Donald repeated. 'Do you know why that was necessary?'

'Yes, I do. Mr Mason told me. She wouldn't hand over the things she stole from his office. Books. Account books.'

'And he asked you to keep her here. Then I take it he doesn't live here? Is that right?'

Fred nodded. 'S'right. He ... Mr Mason ... said to keep her locked up in the cellar until she agreed to give him back his books. That's all I did.'

'Would you please show us this cellar where you kept her,' said Donald rising.

Fred led the way back to the hall where he opened a door to show a flight of wooden stairs leading down. He leaned around the door and turned on the lights.

Donald stepped forward to the top of the stairs, Pat and Hodgkiss crowding behind him.

The cellar was chaotic. Several tall wine racks had been overturned and the bottles smashed. Red wine had pooled in large lakes.

Donald asked. 'And how long did you keep Mrs Field in the cellar.'

'Not long ... couple of days. She was nothing but trouble from the start. She told me to tell Mr Mason that she was going to smash up all the wine unless he let her go.

'And did you pass on that message to Mr Mason.'

'Of course I passed it on.'

'And what did he say?'

'He just told me to tell her that she couldn't go yet. Not till she'd handed over the books. When I told her Mr Mason said she couldn't go she just went ahead and started smashing things up; pushing over the wine racks. Look! You can see for yourselves what she did.'

Donald asked. 'So when she started smashing things up what did you do?'

'I rang Mr Mason straight away and he said to stop her. So I went down and tried to stop her but she hit me with a bottle and scratched my face real bad. I held on to her to try to stop her, that's all. To try to stop her. I held her like that ...'

Here Fred extended both arms rigidly in front of him, fingers curled as if clutching an imaginary throat.

'But it was still no good. She had long arms and she could still reach my face and she was still scratching me.

'Next thing I knew … well … I felt her go sort of heavy as if I was holding her up. And then when I let her go she just fell to the floor.'

Donald asked. 'Then what did you do?'

'I rang Mr Mason of course and told him what had happened and that I thought the lady was dead.'

He paused.

'Go on,' Donald urged. 'What did Mr Mason say?'

'Mr Mason said I'd have to get rid of her. He said she couldn't be found here. He said I should take her to the park just down the road and leave her there. It was still the middle of the night — pitch dark it was — so I took her in the car and left her there out of sight behind a bush. I don't think anyone saw me. I parked where there was no street light and it's pretty dark up there anyway. He said he'd ring the police and tip them off about what they'd find if they went there. He told me he was going to get a message to her husband telling him to go there to meet his wife and then he was going to tip off the police so they'd be there to pick him up when he arrived.'

Donald nodded. 'And after you put her behind the bush you just came on home again, did you?'

'Yes. Then Mr Mason rang again to see that I'd done it right and I told him I had.'

'Thank you, Mr Baker. Now you will have to come with me to the Crestwood Police Station where you will be charged in connection with Mrs Field's death.'

'But I told you,' Fred protested, raising a hand to his wounded face, 'it was self defence. *She'd* have killed *me* if she had the chance. You ask Mr Mason. He'll back up everything I've told you.'

Donald said: 'Oh I'll be asking Mr Mason all right. And I'll be very surprised if he hasn't got a completely different slant on things.'

Fred shot an anxious look in Donald's direction.

Hodgkiss stepped forward. 'Before we go, Donald. I suggest you ask Mr Baker if it was he who burgled Mr Field's home this morning?'

Donald turned to Fred, eye brows raised. 'Well. What about it? Did you?'

Fred shrugged. 'Mrs Field stole the company's account books and Mr Mason wanted me to get them back. He thought they might be there, but they weren't.'

Donald couldn't help but feel a pang of sympathy for the man as he led him out to the unmarked police car parked around the corner.

* * *

'Of course it happened just like I thought. Mason reckoned he never had anything to do with Mrs Field's death.'

Donald, Pat and Hodgkiss were seated around the redwood table on the back deck of the Burke's home conducting a post mortem on the investigation.

'I warned Fred Baker that's what'd happen.'

'Have you charged Mason yet?' Pat asked. 'I mean, he was really behind the whole thing. He arranged the kidnapping and holding her prisoner just so he could to on selling contaminated pills to the public.'

Donald nodded. 'Oh yes. He's been charged too. I went and picked him up after I'd locked Baker up. Of course he denied saying anything to Baker about restraining Mrs Field or keeping her there.'

'What did he expect Baker to do when she started smashing the bottles; appeal to her better nature.'

'Which reminds me,' said Pat, reaching into a deep handbag beside where she was sitting. 'You're going to need these,' she said placing a bulky envelope on the table in front of Donald.

'The cause of all the problems … the company's account books that Frances took off with. She was going to hand them over to the health department. You'd better do it now I suppose.'

'Yeah. I'll hand them over to Superintendent O'Hare and leave him to deal with that side of things. But there's one other little matter I'd like to hear about.'

'Oh, and what's that?' Hodgkiss asked.

'How did the two of you know that they'd been holding her at that particular house in the side street just down the road from the park?'

Pat glanced towards Hodgkiss then said. 'Edgar worked out the address from a text message Frances sent to her husband after they'd locked her in the cellar.'

'You mean they let her keep her phone?' said Donald. 'Not very smart of them.'

'Oh no. They took her phone. You tell him, Edgar. You worked it out.'

Hodgkiss nodded. 'It wasn't all that complicated. Mason wanted her to send a text to her husband saying that everything was fine and not to worry, but she wasn't to send it until Baker had read it over to him and he'd said it was OK to send it. So Baker gave her the phone, watched while she wrote the message, then he read it over to Mason who obviously was elsewhere at the time which was probably just as well since he may have picked up on the grammatical errors and smelled a rat.'

'He probably wouldn't, you know,' said Pat. 'Frances told me he was practically illiterate.'

Donald asked. 'You mean Mason allowed the message to go out saying where she was being held?'

'Yes, but of course he didn't realise that the message contained the address.'

'So how did she do it? What did this miraculous message actually say?'

'Here. I'll show you,' said Pat reaching for her phone and dabbing at the key pad.

She set the phone down before Donald.

'See if you can work it out … spot the address.'

Donald looked at the tiny screen, frowning.

I'm with Mr Mason working on a new project. Its OK so don't you worry or I'll worry to. Sorry. I should of made some dinners for you before I left so go out to a hotel. If you still have the flue take some milk and honey To Ward it of. Don't worry. Their treating me fine. Love Fran.

He said, shaking his head. 'Well, she sure as hell couldn't spell … but I don't see an address anywhere.'

'It wasn't just the spelling that was bad,' said Hodgkiss. 'It was the use of grammar. Appalling! In fact it was so bad that it made Pat and I suspect that the errors were deliberate and therefore designed to get our attention and to turn our minds to a thorough scrutiny of the text.'

'And how did this "thorough scrutiny of the text" come up with an address?'

'It was simple really. Look at the sentence starting "If you still …. etc"'

'Yeah. What about it?'

'Ask yourself why would Frances Field have used capital letters for the words To Ward, which should have been written as one word anyway.'

'I've no idea. You tell me.'

'Very well. Capital letters are used for proper nouns ... place names, for example. Or street names. So Ward could have been Ward Street or Ward Road or Avenue. And the To with a capital letter could, in the context of Ward being a street, be a street number; number Two ... Two Ward Street.'

'But that was all pretty tenuous, wasn't it, Dad? I mean, if I'd known that's all you had to go on I wouldn't have run around the house looking in the windows.'

'Well it's just as well you did. But that wasn't all we had to go on. When Mason rang Bernard Field to set him up at the park in time for the police to arrest him, he gave him a map reference which, fortunately, Bernard wrote on a piece of paper which he left near the street directory on his desk. Once we'd worked out that Ward was a street we checked it in the street directory and we went straight there. The rest you know.'

As Pat reached across the table to recover her phone Donald said: 'And you mean to say you got onto what was happening just because of a couple of mistakes in her message?'

Hodgkiss exploded. '"A couple of mistakes?!" A couple means two, Donald. That message was riddled with errors. There was more than a couple ... many more?'

Donald glanced again at the tiny screen. 'All right, Dad, then how many mistakes d'you think she made?'

'At last count there were nine,' Hodgkiss said emphatically.

'Oh, no,' said Pat quickly. 'I'm sure there were only eight. I went through it carefully. Eight.'

Hodgkiss shook his head. He said, with an effort at

politeness that came out as condescension. 'No, Pat, there were definitely nine errors. I'm counting the capital letters for To and Ward.'

Pat nodded. 'So am I. I still make only eight. I'm not counting "a hotel" as a grammatical error.'

'But of course it is,' Hodgkiss snapped. 'The correct form would have been "an hotel", as well you know

Pat shook her head. 'That's not a grammatical error, Hodgkiss. It's only an matter of usage.'

Donald pushed back his bench. 'What a lot of silly hair-splitting. "An hotel" or "a hotel?" Who cares?'

Hodgkiss shook his head. 'That's typical of you, Donald. Either something is correct or it is not. Now, if you had just taken the trouble to …'

And so the argument rolled on.

Hodgkiss and the Erroneous Email

Ivan Crane swung his chair around to look out the window of his seventh-floor office.

The rain was falling heavily now. This rotten, damp weather played havoc with his chest.

He pushed back his chair, rose and walked out into the lift lobby.

Mary Corbett looked up from behind the reception desk as he approached. She smiled. 'If you're going out you'll need an umbrella, Ivan,' she said.

Ivan shrugged. 'I didn't bring one today. It didn't look like rain when I left home.'

Mary reached down and pulled open the bottom drawer of her desk. 'You can borrow mine. I always keep one here just in case.'

She produced a small umbrella neatly folded into a black sleeve.

'I don't think I'll need it, thanks Mary. I'm not going far. I just need a breath of air.'

He turned and hurried away towards the lifts.

At ground level people were milling at the revolving doors, putting up their umbrellas before venturing into the rain.

Ivan slipped out, but instead of heading for the concrete steps that led down to the footpath, he turned right, hugging the wall to avoid the rain. He had gone no more than ten paces before he slid into one of the series of alcoves created by the unusual design of the office building.

These alcoves were frequently used by employees who, banned from smoking indoors, used them to indulge their vice in secret.

Ivan settled against the concrete wall and took out his asthma puffer.

He shook it and raised it to his mouth.

But before he operated it he heard a voice from the adjoining alcove. Then another voice ... both voices Ivan recognised.

They belonged to Jerry Ferris and Barry Morris, two other employees of the pharmaceutical company where Ivan worked.

Ivan returned the puffer to his pocket without using it. He did not want either of the men in the adjoining space to know of his condition. He had always been embarrassed about using his puffer in public.

Without trying to listen Ivan could not help but hear most of what the two men were saying because they were not speaking in lowered voices as if privacy was important.

He distinctly heard phrases such as 'clinical trials', 'quality controls', 'sterile testing'.

As he listened Ivan's concern mounted from alarm to horror. He had learned matters he would much rather have never known.

It was plain that the two men were planning to enhance the outcome of trials they had been conducting on a new drug that was expected to boost the profile and profitability of their company.

One of the men, Ivan thought the voice was Morris', said: 'If this one goes down the drain we go down the drain with it.'

The other, Ferris, added: 'and so will Forrest. And he's going to be particularly pissed off since we told him in the last report that everything was going great.'

'Well, we're going to have to do a bit of serious revision aren't we,' said Ferris. 'But just the same it isn't going to be like thalidomide … it's not as if taking the stuff is going to actually harm anyone. It wouldn't even give them a headache or a sore throat.'

'No. It's just not going to do anyone much good.'

As company secretary Ivan had known for some time that the company had difficulties with cash-flow. Now problems with the tests on what the company hoped would be its new flagship product …well, that would be the last straw.

But not only that. If what the men in the adjoining alcove were saying was true, as it must be since they were directly involved in the tests they had mentioned, then the company was engaging in a serious fraud.

And if it became public … well, the consequences were too dire to even think about.

His first thought now was how to return to the building and to the safety of his desk without the other men seeing him and knowing that he must have overheard them.

But it was too late. Now they were there, in front of him,

standing in the rain, looking into the alcove where he sheltered.

One of them, Morris, began. 'What the hell …'

But the other, Ferris, cut him off. 'Just popped out for a fag, did you, Ivan?'

'For a fag?' said Morris. 'Not likely. He doesn't smoke. He just popped out for a spot of eavesdropping. Isn't that right, Ivan?'

Ivan could only shake his head.

Then the other two walked off into the rain towards the entry doors.

Ivan remained standing in the alcove. He reached for his puffer again.

*   *   *

As they went up in the lift Morris said: 'Do you think he heard?'

'Of course he bloody heard,' snapped Ferris, 'which gives us a real problem.'

'What do you mean? How is it our problem?'

'Use your brains, mate. If he spills his guts and word gets out about you-know-what, then who do you think is going to get the blame for shooting their mouths off?'

Morris nodded thoughtfully. 'Yeah. I see what you mean. The finger'd be pointed at us because we're the only ones who're supposed to know what's going on with the tests. But what can we do about it?'

'We can take out insurance; that's what we do.'

'Insurance. What do you mean … insurance?'

'By insurance I mean we make sure our backsides are covered if word gets out … if Ivan shoots his mouth off.'

'OK. But why would the little creep tell anyone about it. I mean, if the company goes belly up it's his job on the line too.'

'Yeah. But we've got a lot more to lose than him, right?'

Morris nodded. 'I see what you mean. But what can we do about it?'

'What we can do about it is to tell Arthur what happened … about Ivan eavesdropping on us.'

Morris nodded. 'Yeah. Maybe. But we shouldn't have even been talking about it anyway, should we? We should have been more careful.'

'We thought we were having a private conversation. Right? That's why we went outside … for privacy.'

'Yeah, of course we did. But you know what they say … loose lips sink ships.'

'Loose lips have got nothing to do with it,' Ferris snapped. 'We were discussing ways of getting around a problem. A company problem. Right? That's what we were doing. Talking about work, mate. We weren't to know the creep was spying on us.'

Now they were standing outside the door to the office of Arthur Forrest, general manager of Esoteric Enterprises.

Ferris knocked, pushed the door open and stepped in. He smiled winningly. 'Hello there, Jan.

Until a month ago Jerry Ferris and Jan Evans had been an 'item.' Then Jerry had abruptly switched his attention to a young woman working on the fifth floor.

Jan, headphones covering her ears, looked up from her word processor. She removed one of the headphones.' Yes, Jerry. What is it?' she asked, not pleased with the interruption.

'Is he in?' Ferris asked, tossing his head towards the connecting door to Arthur Forrest's office.

'He's in, but he's in conference at the moment. Do you want to wait?'

'Will he be long, do you think? It's pretty important. Urgent, really.'

'He shouldn't be long. Take a seat.' She adjusted the head-phones, but instead of resuming typing she began to pore over a document on the desk beside her word processor.

The two men sat in low chrome-plated chairs near Forrest's office door.

Ferris began softly. 'What we've got to do is simply tell him the facts … what happened exactly. No harm in that. Bloody Ivan had no business being there. We'll keep it simple. It's Ivan's doing if word gets out … not ours.'

Morris shook his head. 'Do you reckon Forrest will go for that? I mean it's our problem really isn't it. Who's fiddling the whole process? That's the real problem … right?'

'Yeah, but you've got to keep your mouth shut about that. It's jail time if that ever comes out. Besides that's something the creep hasn't got a clue about. All he knows is that the results aren't looking great at this stage of the game. That's all we said out there, and that's all we tell Forrest.'

'But he knows that already. We said that in our report to him last week.'

Ferris hesitated. 'Yeah, maybe. But not in so many words.'

'But I said it … in my report. I made a point of telling him things weren't looking great. You read it.'

'I read something like that. But I didn't think the timing was right to put it in black and white to the top brass, not as bluntly as you put it. We've still got plenty of time to sort things out, right. So we've just got to hold our nerve and no one will know. We did what we had to do to keep the show on the road. Nobody's going to blame us for that … particularly Forrest with all the shares he owns in the company.'

'So what you're telling me is that you haven't told Forrest about the tests ... the problems we're having.'

'He knows there's *a* problem. I just didn't make it sound quite as bad as you did in your report. That's all.'

'So exactly how did you put it?'

Just then the door to Forrest's office opened and Forrest appeared, fare-welling a tall, blonde woman.

'Then I'll be in touch soon, Arthur,' the woman said, shaking a proffered hand.

'As soon as you like, my dear,' said Forrest, before turning his attention to Ferris and Morris.

'And how can I help you two?' he asked.

'Just a few words, Arthur,' said Ferris. 'Nothing to worry about ... really.'

When the office door closed behind them Jan removed the headphones, picked up her mobile and thumbed the keypad.

'I just heard something you'll want to know,' she began.

It was not a long conversation and when Jan finished she replaced the headphones, this time adjusting them properly to cover her ears.

*   *   *

'So what is it?' Forrest was behind his desk, the other two seated opposite.

Ferris glanced at Morris then began. 'Neither of us enjoys telling tales on a fellow employee, but I think we've got no choice in the circumstances.'

'OK, Jerry, what's happened?' Forrest asked, prepared for the worst.

'Just now Barry and I went downstairs for a breath of fresh

air and to talk over a few things in private. You know what it's like in the office … all open plan. No privacy. Anyway, we were standing talking in one of those alcoves around the outside of the building.'

Forrest knew of these smokers' havens. He nodded. 'Yeah, I know where you mean. Go on.'

'Anyway, when we'd finished talking and were coming back inside we came across Ivan Crane. He was standing in the next alcove. We think he'd been eavesdropping on us … deliberately. Well, we know he had. You could see from the guilty look on his face.'

'Is that so?' asked Forrest, unimpressed. 'And what did he hear that's got you worried enough to come and tell me about it?'

'Nothing you don't already know, Arthur.'

'Is it about the Bulmer programme?'

Jerry nodded. 'Yes. But like I said, it's nothing for you to worry about.'

'But you still wanted to tell me about it … about Crane overhearing you?'

'Yes, just in case people start talking … that's all. You know how things are in this business … how everyone gossips.'

Forrest looked from one to the other. 'Yeah. I know all about that. Now is there something else you should be telling me? I read that report of yours last week about Bulmer. From reading that there's nothing to worry about. Right? Bulmer's going according to plan?'

Ferris managed a smile. 'All going to plan,' he echoed.

Forrest nodded. 'Right. I've heard what you had to say. Let's hope that's the end of it.' He paused, then continued. 'You two don't like Crane very much, do you?'

Ferris shrugged. 'It's not a matter of liking him or not liking him. I think he's weird … strange. Not … you know … quite normal.'

'In what way exactly,' Forrest asked.

'Well for a start he's on tranquilizers,' said Ferris, improvising. 'I suppose that's why he never seems to be quite with it. And he was supposed to have had a nervous break-down last year. That's when he took his holidays. I understand he never went to New Zealand like he said, but he spent most of his time in a private hospital.'

'And did he … is that true?' Forrest asked.

'I couldn't say,' said Ferris. 'I didn't follow it up. I wasn't all that interested.'

Forrest rose. 'I'll bear in mind what you've told me.'

When the two were gone Forrest swung his chair around to face the window. He looked out at the rain.

He thought: those two must think I came down in the last shower.

Arthur Forrest was not a trusting soul. He had his own ways of keeping track of the company's various testing programmes without the testing staff knowing about it.

He was painfully aware that the tests on one of the company's most promising new products, Bulmer, a diet pill, were not shaping up.

Forrest knew, too, that the company's survival depended on the success of Bulmer. An expensive advertising programme had been commissioned from his cousin's advertising agency and there was no going back on that.

Drastic situations required drastic measures.

*   *   *

As the two passed through the outer office Ferris stopped at Jan Evans' desk. 'See you at lunchtime in the canteen?'

But Jan did not bother to look up. She continued typing, headphones now firmly in place.

'Bitch,' Ferris muttered as the two headed for the lifts.

The office door had scarcely closed behind the two men when Jan's phone buzzed.

'Yes, Mr Forrest?'

'Will you find me the number for Mr Voce. I seem to have mislaid it.'

As she scrolled through her menu of phone numbers Jan recalled Mr Voce ... Mr. Ken Voce, to be exact.

After Voce's last meeting with Arthur Forrest, Jan had made a few discreet inquiries about Voce and had not been surprised to learn that he had the reputation of a vicious stand-over man.

Her informant had been a senior detective she was dating at the time. The detective had been surprised to learn that the chief executive of a reputable pharmaceutical company should feel the need to contact a person like Voce, a man with an extensive criminal record.

But that had been several years ago, the detective told Jan. Voce had not been in trouble recently, so perhaps his circumstances had changed, but somehow he doubted it. The detective ventured the opinion that Mr Voce was the kind of leopard who was not likely to change his spots: tall-ish, dark-haired and thick-set, with the rough tongue of an uneducated man.

Jan Evans found Voce's number and read it over to Mr Forrest. Then she got up from her desk, crossed to her door. closed it, then went to the door to Mr Forrest's office.

She leaned forward to listen, careful to keep an eye on her

own door to the corridor.

When Forrest had finished his phone call he buzzed through to Jan's desk again.

'Jan would you bring me that copy of the staff magazine from last month … the one with the photos from the staff Christmas Party in it.'

'Yes, Mr Forrest, I know the one you mean. I have a copy on my file.'

*   *   *

Jan Evans had been sitting in an out-of-the-way table in the canteen only minutes before Mary Corbett arrived.

'So what's the drama?' Mary asked as soon as she had taken her seat opposite the other woman.

'It's something I think you should know about,' Jan said. 'It's about Ivan.'

Mary Corbett had made no secret of her feelings for Ivan Crane although Ivan had made no response to some rather obvious advances.

'What's happened to Ivan now?' Mary asked anxiously.

Jan asked cautiously. 'Did he go out of the office for a while this morning.'

Mary nodded. 'Yes. Why? What did he do?'

'I don't think it's anything he did,' said Jan. 'It's more a case of what some other people think he might do.'

Mary said. 'I noticed when he came back he looked rather upset about something. I tried to speak to him but he walked right past my desk like a zombie.'

Jan nodded. 'Well, that figures. What happened was that Ferris and Morris from the lab went downstairs not long before Ivan and when he sheltered from the rain in one of those little bays at ground level he overheard what they were talking about because they were in the next bay, or they assumed he overheard them. And because of what they think he heard they're worried that he could make one hell of a problem for them if he ever decided to talk about it. As soon as they came back upstairs they went to see Forrest. I overheard some of what they were talking about before they went in to see him. They thought I had my headphones on but they weren't in my ears. From what I heard they were scared stiff that Ivan heard them talking about how one of their testing programmes has gone badly off the rails and they could be in big trouble over it. But worse than that, they mentioned that they'd been rigging the results.'

'No wonder the poor fellow seemed worried sick when he came back,' said Mary. 'They're real wheeler-dealers, those two … aren't they; Ferris and Morris. They wouldn't be taking the blame if any of their programmes went wrong … not if they could pass it on to someone else.'

'Unfortunately that's not all,' said Jan. 'I listened in to their meeting with Forrest and they told him that Ivan had been deliberately easvesdropping on them and that if anything came out about the test not showing good results then it'd be Ivan that blew the whistle, not them. Then as soon as they came out of Forrest's office he rang and asked me to get a particular phone number for him. The number for a fellow called Ken Voce.'

Mary shook her head. 'I don't think I've heard of anyone of that name before. Certainly Ivan has never mentioned him.'

'No. He wouldn't have. Voce doesn't work for us. Actually, from what I've heard, he's a kind of stand-over man … a thug … a hardened criminal.'

Mary looked shocked. 'A stand-over man. But what would Mr Forrest be doing speaking to someone like that?'

'A very good question, Mary,' said Jan. 'Of course I don't know what they spoke about because Forrest rang Voce on his mobile, but look at the timing; Ferris and Morris go into the office, they tell Forrest about Ivan overhearing what they were talking about … something that could mean really big trouble for the company if word gets out. Then as soon as the two of them come out of the office Forrest rings a standover man. And what's more as soon as Forrest had finished on that call he rang me to get a copy of our staff magazine with photos from the Christmas Party in it. I checked before I took it in to him … there's a big photo of Ivan in it because he was one of the organisers.'

'But Ivan couldn't help it if he happened to be downstairs and heard what those two were saying … things he knew nothing about.'

Jan nodded agreement. 'Of course he couldn't help it. But whatever those two told Forrest it certainly put the wind up him. They must have convinced him that Ivan knew enough to jeopardise the project if he shot his mouth off. They said he'd had a few problems in the past. They tried to make him sound like a psychiatric case. I heard them telling Forrest that Ivan had a nervous breakdown but said he'd gone on holidays to cover it up although he was actually in hospital.'

'But that's ridiculous,' said Mary. 'He had to take a few days off because he had a particularly bad bout of asthma. Ivan would never do anything to harm the reputation of the company.'

'No, of course he wouldn't. But I just thought you should know what's happened; what those two told Forrest, and maybe warn Ivan to be on the lookout.'

'On the lookout! How can someone like Ivan be on the lookout against a stand-over man ... a thug? Ivan's not a well man with his asthma.'

'I know,' said Jan. 'But I thought I'd let you know about it'

*　*　*

When five o'clock came Ivan waited until most of the others in his office had left before he gathered his papers, locked them away in his desk, then went out to the lift.

At the ground floor he found Mary Corbett waiting just outside the main doors.

The rain had stopped and a watery sun had appeared. Mary smiled as he approached. 'No need for a brolly now,' she said.

When Ivan said nothing she continued. 'Ivan, there's something I need to talk to you about.'

She could not miss the flicker of alarm that fleeted across his face.

She continued determinedly. 'When you went out this morning for a breather something happened to upset you, didn't it, Ivan?'

For a moment Ivan recalled his horror at being discovered in the alcove by the two men, but it was not something that he wanted to discuss or to dwell on.

'No, nothing happened ... nothing at all,' he said unconvincingly.

Mary shook her head. 'There's no reason why you shouldn't tell me about it, Ivan. I think I know what happened anyway.'

'No,' said Ivan, now distressed. 'You can't possibly know. I mean, how could you? You weren't there.'

'Never mind how I know. I can't tell you anyway, because

someone else is involved. But I know it was something to do with Ferris and Morris, the two fellows from Testing.'

When Ivan said nothing she continued.

'You overheard something they said about a problem with one of their important programmes and they saw you and thought you'd been deliberately eavesdropping on them.'

'But I wasn't,' Ivan cried, near tears. 'I wasn't eavesdropping. I wouldn't do that.'

'No of course you wouldn't. You wouldn't do a thing like that, I know.'

'But how do you know about it … about what happened?'

'I'm sorry, Ivan. I can't say … not yet anyway … but I believe what I was told and I'm sure you did nothing wrong. It was just unfortunate you were there at the same time as those two.'

'I couldn't help it. I would have explained it to them, but I never had a chance. They thought I'd gone there to deliberately spy on them and listen in on what they were saying. But how could I. I had no idea they were there until I got there myself. I was feeling a bit wheezy and had gone downstairs to use my puffer. Then I heard them. They weren't whispering or anything like that. They were talking in quite normal voices so I couldn't help hearing every word they said. Then I was afraid that if I tried to come away and go back inside they might hear me or see me, so I just stayed there and hoped they'd leave and walk past without looking in and seeing me.'

He paused and turned to her. 'But they did. They saw me there. What can I do? Should I go and try to talk to them and let them know that I won't tell anyone what I heard?'

Mary shook her head. 'I don't think that would help now. I'm afraid that things have moved on too far for something like that.'

'What do you mean?' said Ivan, alarmed, '"moved on too far?"'

'I can only tell you what I've heard from someone I know and trust, and that is that Ferris and Morris went straight to Mr Forrest's office when they came upstairs and told him about what happened.'

'And I suppose they said that I'd deliberately gone down there to spy on them.'

'Yes. I'm told that's exactly what they said.'

'But surely Mr Forrest wouldn't believe it just because they told him. Surely he'd want to talk to me too … ask me for my side of it before he'd believe anything those two said about me.'

'You'd think so, wouldn't you, but I'm afraid that's not what's happened. Unfortunately it seems that he believed them … which I think was very wrong of him.'

'But how do you know this. How do you know he believed them?'

'Look, Ivan. I've told you what I know. I'm sorry that I can't tell you who told me, but I promise you that the person is very reliable and she … she's no friend of that pair from Testing.'

'And is that where it's at now … Mr Forrest thinks I've somehow found out that one of our testing programmes has been compromised and that I'm going to turn whistleblower and make trouble for the company?'

Mary shook her head. 'No, Ivan. I'm afraid that's not all there is. It's worse than that.'

'Worse! How could it possibly be any worse?'

'Mr Forrest has hired a strong-arm man … a thug, and now he's got hold of a photo of you in a back issue of the staff magazine. And the only reason I can think of for him getting hold of your photo is so this thug can identify you.'

Ivan shook his head in bewilderment. 'This is too much. I don't believe it. It just can't be true. Please tell me this is a practical joke.'

'No, Ivan,' Mary said, upset now. 'I'd never be so cruel as to tell you something like this if I didn't know it was true.'

'But if it's really true what can I do about it? Should I go and hide somewhere. I can't go home, can I, if this man is looking for me. Should I ring the police? What?'

'Do you have any holidays owing?'

Ivan nodded. 'Yes. I've got months of leave owing.'

'Then I think you should take it. If you can't stay at home then stay at a friend's place if possible. You could stay with me if you want to. I've got a spare room. Meanwhile my friend and I will keep an ear to the ground and see what happens next. Perhaps we can keep track of whatever they're planning to do.'

Ivan shrugged. 'Well, I suppose it's the best I can do for the present. Thank you, Mary. I won't stay any longer than I have to. I don't want to be a nuisance.'

Mary smiled and took his hand. 'Don't worry, Ivan. You won't be a nuisance.'

* * *

Edgar Hodgkiss pulled back the heavy sliding door from the family room and stepped out onto the back deck.

His dog, Rupert, a small animal of indeterminate breed, scampered up the short flight of wooden steps from the driveway at the side of the house.

Hodgkiss slipped the harness over Rupert's head, attached the lead and the two set off down the driveway and into the street.

As they walked Hodgkiss thoughts turned to the rather odd man who he had encountered on their walks recently.

Hodgkiss was a creature of very fixed habits. He had been taking Rupert for morning walks for several years now. The walks always began with Hodgkiss making three circuits of the nearby oval where Rupert was freed from the lead to socialize with the other dogs who came there regularly with their owners.

Then, after the regulation three circuits, the two set off on a well-trodden route which involved two blocks of fairly level walking before turning for home.

During the course of these walks Hodgkiss and Rupert met, at various predictable points along their way, other walkers, some with dogs some without, who followed a similar exercise routine.

But during the past few weeks a new walker had appeared on their route; Hodgkiss had dubbed him Mr Anxious because of his wary demeanour.

He was a fellow of about forty, Hodgkiss judged, and since he walked the route in the opposite direction to Hodgkiss, they always encountered each other head on.

The man usually avoided eye-contact with Hodgkiss and on one occasion he had stepped pointedly to one side as Hodgkiss approached as if fearing some form of unwelcome familiarity.

Once Hodgkiss raised a hand in friendly greeting as the man approached, but he had responded only with a flap of a wrist as he hurried by, eyes averted.

On another occasion Hodgkiss had seen a small blue sedan, driven by a rather attractive youngish woman, stop at the kerb and the man had got in and been driven away.

As he turned a corner which marked the furthest point of

their route, Hodgkiss saw Mr Anxious approaching dressed in his usual turnout of black tracksuit pants, white shirt with a Latin slogan which Hodgkiss was unable to translate, and orange trainers, obviously new.

As the gap between the two closed Hodgkiss prepared to make an attempt at casual conversation, possibly relating to the weather since it was certainly a fine morning and the electronic sign outside the school nearby showed the temperature at a pleasant 18 degrees.

But before Hodgkiss could make his opening remarks he noticed a large black sedan come to an abrupt halt just ahead of where Mr Anxious was walking. Both front doors flew open and two men tumbled out.

The man who had alighted from the nearside door, a tall thickset man with dark hair, made straight for Mr Anxious, apparently bent on some kind of confrontation. The other man, the driver, who was short and bald, was around the car quickly, obviously with every intention of assisting with whatever his passenger had in mind.

As Hodgkiss drew near the intention of the two men was plain; they were attempting to force Mr Anxious into their car and Mr Anxious was resisting their efforts vigourously but obviously in vain.

Hodgkiss dropped Rupert's lead and walked quickly forward.

'And what do you two think you're playing at,' he demanded. 'Let that fellow go.'

'You mind your own business, Pops,' said the bald man. 'You'll keep out of this if you know what's good for you.'

'I've never known what's good for me,' said Hodgkiss, taking the phone from his slacks pocket and switching it to camera mode.

He raised the phone and there was a flash, then another and another.

The dark man released his grip on Mr Anxious and turned to Hodgkiss. 'Hey you, what the hell do you think you're doing?'

Hodgkiss replied. 'I am simply making a record of what is undoubtedly an attempted abduction and a criminal assault.'

'You're a real smart arse, aren't you?' said the man, advancing with menace. 'Give me that thing here,' he said.

Hodgkiss turned and flung the phone over a nearby hedge into the front garden of a rather imposing two-storey home.

'And if you want to retrieve it you will add trespass to your list of offences?' he added.

'We'll see about that,' said the dark man heading for the gate to the property.

But Rupert was ahead of him, his lead trailing on the ground behind him as he dashed around the hedge.

Hodgkiss turned back to where the bald man was still grappling ineffectually with Mr Anxious.

He took a tiny pad with a built-in pencil from his shirt pocket then walked to the front of the car and began rather ostentatiously to make a note of the registration number.

'And what the hell's that about?' demanded the bald man, releasing his hold on Mr Anxious. 'You can't just go about writing down people's car numbers.'

'I most certainly can,' said Hodgkiss, 'particularly in circumstances where the occupants of the vehicle are committing serious criminal offences.'

'Nobody's committed any offences,' the bald man argued.

'I disagree,' said Hodgkiss. 'You were undoubtedly attempting to abduct this man.' He turned to Mr Anxious who was hovering nearby. 'Isn't that so? Were those men trying to force you into their car?'

Mr Anxious nodded. 'Yes.'

'And you didn't want to go, did you?'

'No. I don't even know them. And I certainly didn't want to go anywhere with them.'

Any further discussion was interrupted by a volley of barking and shouting from the far side of the hedge.

Then there was a squeal followed by a roar of rage and moments later the dark man returned with Hodgkiss' phone in one hand and a bloody handkerchief wrapped around the other.

'That bloody animal bit me,' he said. 'I could have him put down.'

'I'd say you got what you deserved,' Hodgkiss said.

As the man approached Hodgkiss put out a hand. 'And I'll have my phone back, thank you very much.'

'D'you reckon,' said the dark man. He raised the phone high over his head then dashed it down on the footpath where it shattered.

'There. *Now* you can have it back,' he said. He turned to his companion. 'C'mon. let's get out of here.'

Indicating Hodgkiss the bald man said to his partner: 'He wrote down our number plate.'

'Did he indeed,' the dark man said, advancing on Hodgkiss. 'And what did you do that for?'

'So that you can be identified of course,' Hodgkiss explained unnecessarily. 'You don't seriously think that I am just about to forget what has happened here, do you? The police will be following his matter up. You may be sure of that. Now, in addition to attempted abduction, assault and trespass you also face a charge of causing willful damage to property ... my phone.'

He added casually. 'Since the two of you are very likely well known to the police you may know my son-in-law, Detective Inspector Donald Burke. He's stationed at Crestwood. Nice and handy to begin an investigation into your little crime spree.'

Whether or not either of the men recognised Donald's name Hodgkiss could not tell, but upon hearing this information both men returned quickly to their car, started up and sped away.

Hodgkiss turned to where Mr Anxious stood leaning against a power pole, a puffer to his mouth.

'Have you any idea why those men were trying to kidnap you?' he asked.

Mr Anxious nodded, then administered another puff.

'When your breathing has settled down perhaps you would be so good as to enlighten me. By the way, my name's Hodgkiss, Edgar Hodgkiss.

The other man put the puffer in his tracksuit pocket. He held out a hand. 'Ivan Crane,' he said. 'And thanks for coming along when you did, otherwise ... well, I don't know what they would have done to me.'

'But who were they, and why did they want to kidnap you? They must be rather desperate for your company to try to drag you off the streets in broad daylight like that.'

'Yes, I suppose they must be.'

'So what's it all about. Are you going to tell me?'

'I don't think I'd be doing you any favours if I told you because then you might somehow become mixed up in my problem.'

'Well, Mr Crane, I am already mixed up in your problem. What I said about my son-in-law being a detective was not a story I made up on the spur of the moment to scare those thugs away. It happens to be perfectly true and I will certainly be reporting to him everything that took place here, so I'd say that I'm involved already. So you might as well tell me exactly what it's all about. I may be in a position to help.'

'Very well, Edgar. But first let me ring my friend to come and collect me. She lives very close by and I'd rather not walk home just now. Those two fellows could still be hanging around somewhere waiting to try again. Perhaps you'd like to come along with me and bring your little dog. I'll tell you all about it when we get home.'

Ivan took a phone from his tracksuit pants and jabbed the keypad. 'Mary, would you mind coming to collect me please. There's been a ... a problem. There's a fellow here with me. I'd like to bring him home if that's all right. I owe him an explanation ... more than just an explanation really. Yes. I'll tell you all about it. Thanks.'

Ivan cut the connection. 'I'm sorry about what happened to your phone. It would never have been smashed if ...'

'Don't worry about it, Ivan,' said Hodgkiss, stooping to pick up the remains of his phone. 'Who knows, some of the scientific boys at the police lab might be able to do something with it ... recover the pictures at least.'

They had been waiting only a few minutes before the small blue sedan, driven by the same woman Hodgkiss had seen before, came slowly towards them and pulled to the kerb.

*   *   *

Mary Corbett, this is Edgar Hodgkiss. Edgar probably saved my life.'

From the back seat Hodgkiss wriggled in embarrassment. 'I think that's rather over-stating things, Ivan,' he said.

'You wouldn't say that if you knew the history of this awful business, Mr Hodgkiss,' said Mary.

'I don't say those men *would* have killed Ivan, but they certainly would have made things very unpleasant for him.

'Ivan will tell you all about it when we get home.'

Home was a flat on the ground floor of an old fashion two storey building near the Kylerbrin Railway Station.

When the three were settled in the kitchen with mugs of coffee and hot buttered toast Mary began.

'It all started less than a month ago, although it seems much longer. Ivan works for a pharmaceutical company. He's not a chemist … not on the scientific side. He's the company secretary. He has to keep track of all their expenditure and make sure that all the customers pay up on time and generally keep the financial wheels turning.

'Anyway, as you may have noticed, he suffers with his chest, quite badly at times, and one morning he went downstairs from the office to use his puffer … he doesn't like using it in front of other people, particularly the people at work.

'The building where we work is one of these very modern-looking ones and at ground level, because of the way the it's built, there are all these little separate alcoves made by the concrete sections. When he goes downstairs to use his puffer he just slips into one of these because they're quite private. I know all this because we work in the same building.'

'For the same company?' Hodgkiss asked.

Mary nodded. 'Yes. I'm the receptionist. I work in the front office.'

'So you would see everyone coming and going.'

'Yes. Anyway, on this day when Ivan went downstairs he slipped into one of these little concrete alcoves or bays in the building to use his puffer, then almost at once he heard two men talking in the next bay. He knew at once who they were and he could hear them quite clearly because they weren't taking any trouble to keep their voices down.

'Anyway, to cut a long story short, he heard them discussing a particular testing programme that's going on at the moment and it was quite clear from what they were saying that the programme is not being conducted properly ... that is ethically.'

'Do you mean that they were planning to misrepresent the results ...to cheat?' Hodgkiss asked

'Yes, that's it exactly. The tests were not turning out as hoped and if the particular programme they were working on has to be abandoned it will be a big blow to the company which is in trouble anyway, according to Ivan.'

Ivan nodded. 'Their cash flow situation is dire. They will have to make serious retrenchments soon if they are to survive. Anyway, as soon as these fellows had finished their discussion they came out to go back inside and unfortunately they saw me right next to where they'd been talking. They knew I must have heard them.'

Hodgkiss said. 'And they thought you were going to blow the whistle on the company. Is that it?'

'Yes, but I'd never even thought of telling anyone.'

'And I take it these two men who saw you are responsible for this particular testing programme.'

'Yes. They're two of the lead technicians and they're responsible for all of our important work. I couldn't believe what I was hearing.'

'And from what you heard there was no doubt they were rigging the test results, or intended to.'

'Yes. But of course I don't know how long they'd been there talking before I arrived, so I only heard part of what they were saying. But from what I heard there was no doubt that they were very worried about the results so far. They spoke about serious revision and having to make it look good. They seemed to justify what they were doing by saying that if the drug went on the market it wouldn't actually harm anyone who took it, but it wouldn't do them any good either.'

Hodgkiss asked. 'And when they saw you, what did they do? Did they confront you about it and try to persuade you to hold your tongue? Did they threaten you … try to bribe you?'

Mary shook her head. 'No. They didn't do anything like that. When they came back inside they went straight to their boss, Mr Forrest, and reported what had happened, but in such a way that it looked like Ivan had gone down there to deliberately spy on them.'

'And what did this Mr Forrest do? Did he believe them?'

'Yes,' said Ivan. 'That's the worst, most hurtful part. He didn't even ask to see me and give me a chance to explain what had happened. He just went ahead and arranged for those two fellows you saw today to attack me.'

'That seems a very drastic step for him to take,' said Hodgkiss. 'But how could you possibly know that he'd done that?'

'A friend of Mary's who works for Mr Forrest knew about it. She said that Forrest had asked her to get the phone number for a particularly person who is known as a thug and stand-over man.'

'I don't suppose you'd have this fellow's name?'

''Yes. His name is Ken Voce.'

'Excellent. I'll see if Donald is familiar with Mr Voce. If he is all you say he is then I've no doubt he'll have a lengthy entry in the State's criminal records system.'

'And another thing,' said Ivan, 'Mr Forrest asked his girl to get a back issue of the staff magazine with my photo in it, no doubt so the thug could identify me.'

Hodgkiss stood up. 'Well, I'd say we have enough information to lay before my son-on-law in the hope that he will see fit to take the matter seriously and begin an investigation. But I must warn you now that Donald is sometimes a little difficult to prod into action. Now I had better be getting home.'

'I'll give you a lift if you like,' said Mary.

Hodgkiss held up a hand. 'No need for that, thank you, Mary. It's only a hop, step and a jump from here to home. Besides, Rupert didn't get his full walk this morning. He won't be happy.'

And so the two set off home, Hodgkiss turning over in his mind the best avenue of attack in the coming battle to persuade Donald to investigate the rather dramatic events of the morning.

*   *   *

'Where on earth have you been, Dad,' said Esme Burke. 'I was just getting worried about you. You're not usually gone nearly this long.'

Esme, Hodgkiss daughter, was liable to fuss over her father as his years advanced. 'You've got your phone with you, haven't you. Why didn't you ring and let me know? That's why we bought it for you.'

Hodgkiss produced the plastic bag Ivan had given him to carry his shattered phone home with him.

'I couldn't very well ring you with that, could I?' he said upending the bag and allowing the debris to fall out on the kitchen bench.

'And how did you manage to do that?' Esme asked unsympathetically.

'I didn't do it. It was smashed by a very unpleasant man … a thug.'

'A thug! What on earth have you been up to, Dad?'

'What have *I* been up to? Why is it *my* fault if someone hoodlum takes it into his head to smash my phone?'

'It's usually your fault when something like this happens because you can't help interfering in matters that don't concern you.'

'You mean in matters like a man being attacked by two thugs who were obviously trying to abduct him.'

'Oh come on, Dad. You don't expect me to believe that.'

'Esme, I don't care if you believe me or not, and I suspect that Donald's reaction will be the same. Nevertheless I will do what I can to convince him to take me seriously. And failing that I will have to take my concerns to a higher authority.'

Esme rounded on him. 'Don't you dare go behind his back to Superintendent O'Hare like you did last time. He's never forgiven you for that and nor have I.'

'Then let us hope he is prepared to listen to what I have to say and to take it seriously. After all, he doesn't have to accept what I tell him. There's the unfortunate man who was assaulted and nearly kidnapped … I assume Donald will take it seriously if he makes an official complaint about what happened to him this morning.'

'And who's that?'

'Esme, if I am to recount what happened I would prefer to do it while Donald is present so I do not have to go through the whole rigmarole twice. Is he still at home?'

'Yes. He's having his shower. I'll let him know you're back,' said Esme, heading for the hall.

Minutes later she returned with Donald, wrapped in an old tartan dressing gown held together with a cord ending in frayed tassels.

'Reporting a kidnapping this time, are you, Dad?' he asked cheerfully. 'Well, it's a welcome change from murder.'

'Please, Donald, do not make light of this matter.' Hodgkiss said. 'I am talking about attempted abduction, assault, trespass and,' with a hand indicating the shattered mobile phone, 'willful damage to property.'

'Well, you might have a case for the last one.'

'There is a strong case for all four if you bother to listen to the facts and when take them seriously.'

Donald slid into one side of the built-in pine breakfast nook. 'OK, Dad. Let's hear it, but make it snappy, I've got to get to work.'

'This *is* work, Donald. Important work,' said Hodgkiss slipping into the seat opposite Donald. 'It is serious crime. That *is* your line of work, isn't it?'

Donald gritted his teeth. 'Just get on with it, Dad.'

'There's not a great deal to tell. I was walking with Rupert as usual this morning and I saw two men jump out of a car and attempt to force a man into it. Luckily I was able to deter them from this course by capturing their activities on the camera in my phone. When one of them disapproved of this and attempted to take the phone from me I tossed it into the front yard of a nearby home. However he recovered it and smashed it, as you see. When your scientific people have recovered the images I took then we will know the identity of these vicious men.'

Donald glanced at the phone. 'You have to be kidding me. No one's going to be able to recover anything from that wreck.'

'Possibly,' Hodgkiss conceded, 'nevertheless I suggest you give it to your experts to see what they can do.'

'OK. And why were these fellows attacking the other bloke?'

'I suggest you ask him rather than get it third hand from me, but I can certainly give you an outline.'

Donald nodded. "Then let's hear it and I can decide it there's anything worth following up.'

'Donald, I assure you that there is a great deal worth following up. For a start, have you heard the name Ken Voce? I'd hazard a guess that you may find many entries under that name in your criminal records system.'

'Oh yeah. I know all about Ken Voce. A very nasty violent piece of work is Ken. But I think he is inside at the moment.'

Hodgkiss shook his head. 'No, Donald. He is not inside at the moment. He is outside. Very much outside and very active. Now, to continue; the two criminals I have mentioned arrived at and departed from the scene in a vehicle bearing this registration number.'

Hodgkiss slid a page taken from his notebook across the table to Donald who glanced at the number.

'OK, Dad. So what was it all about? Do you know why were they trying to grab this guy off the street?'

'Of course I know what it was all about. The man who these thugs tried to abduct works for a pharmaceutical company. No doubt the two thugs were employed by one of the senior officers of the company who thought that the victim had come into possession of information that he could use to the detriment of the company if he chose to do so.'

'And you think they wanted him kidnapped to shut him up.'

'Do you seriously expect me to be able to answer that? I know none of the people involved except the fellow who was attacked and a young woman who works for the company as their receptionist.

'If you want answers to questions like that you will have to interview those behind the abduction … senior people in the company who had most to lose if the whistle was blown on their corrupt practices.'

'Now we've got "corrupt practices" too, have we?' Donald said, making no attempt to hide his skepticism.

'Yes, Donald. Corrupt practices is what this is all about; dishonest people fiddling the results of tests on chemical products that may one day be sold to unsuspecting members of the public; to you, to Esme … even to me.

'However, that aspect of the matter can wait. For the present I think the best starting point for your investigation would be for you to interview Mr Ivan Crane, on whom the abduction attempt was made.

'If you agree I will ask Mr Crane to present himself at your office tomorrow afternoon for interview. Does that suit?'

Donald shrugged. 'I suppose so, although it'll probably turn out to be a complete and utter waste of police time.'

Late the following afternoon, just as Hodgkiss was about to start on his afternoon tea, a mug of coffee and two shortbread biscuits which Esme had just set down before him on the round redwood table on the back deck, the replacement phone which Esme had loaned him, rang in his shirt pocket.

He took out the phone and opened the connection. 'Yes, Donald. What is it?'

'Your friend Crane never showed. Not that I'm surprised.'

Hodgkiss frowned. 'This is cause for concern, Donald, not for point scoring. I will make inquiries and call you back.'

'Don't bother, Dad. Obviously he's not terribly worried about what happened … allegedly happened … or he would have turned up; or at least rung. He can't be too worried about being abducted again.'

Hodgkiss ended the call and rung a mobile number Mary Corbett had given him.

'Ivan didn't show at the police station,' he said when Mary answered. 'Do you know why?'

Mary sounded concerned. 'No. But I'm terribly worried because he's been gone for most of the day. He left here about nine to do some shopping and he hasn't come back. I thought perhaps he'd have a bite to eat then go straight down to the police station and try to get the interview over early or to make some other arrangement. I would have driven him down to Crestwood but he said not to bother. I hope nothing's happened to him.'

'So do I,' said Hodgkiss. 'If you haven't heard from him within an hour, ring me, please.'

It was just on an hour when the phone rang again. 'I still haven't heard from him. I've rung his phone a dozen times but it's turned off and that's something he never does. I'm really worried, Edgar. What should we do? Would your son-in-law be able to help us?'

'Oh he'd be *able* to help us, but I don't think there's a snowflake's chance in hell that he will … not yet anyway. I've already outlined the situation to him and he seems to regard it as trivial. I fear there is no likelihood whatever of him taking an intelligent interest in the matter for the present, but I will make another attempt.'

*   *   *

Many people, when they are knocked unconscious by a blow to the head, cannot at first remember what happened.

This was not the case with Ivan Crane.

He remembered setting off from the Kylerbrin Mall to walk back to Mary Corbett's flat. He remembered turning the corner from Ireland Street into Foster Street where she lived.

He remembered walking past the house on the corner which had a garage with a sliding door that was set right on the footpath, and he remembered the scuffling noise behind him moments before the blow fell.

He decided that the man or men who attacked him must have been hiding down the side of the garage and waited until after he walked past.

No doubt those responsible were the two men who now sat either side of him in the back of the strange sedan which now, almost incredibly, was driving slowly down a street which, he knew, joined at a right angle to the street where he had lived as a child, up to the age of six.

Just then the car turned into the driveway of a property which Ivan clearly recognised as number nine Polk Close.

His best friend from primary school, Walter Sherring, had lived at number seven, a strange little house with a dwarf turret at the front, which he could now see as the car drove slowly down the driveway at the side of number nine.

'Hello, the sleeping beauty's awake,' said the man on Ivan's left, who he recognised as the dark man who had tried to force him into the car.

The other man, the bald man, said: 'D'you reckon he knows where he is? Perhaps we should have blindfolded him just in case, like the boss said.'

'Nah,' said the dark man. 'Don't worry About it. He was out like a light for most of the way. He'd be just as lost as I am.'

'Where am I?' Ivan asked, just to put the question beyond doubt.

'Never mind where you are, mate,' said the bald man. 'It's where you're going that you need to worry about.'

Ivan looked down. His hands, bound at the wrist with wide black tape, rested in his lap.

Then the car stopped in a rusty carport, overgrown with vines, at the rear of the house.

The two men climbed out and the bald man held the rear door open and helped Ivan to alight.

'Where are you taking me?' he asked, without any hope of receiving an encouraging reply.

Nor did he receive one. The dark man said: 'You'll find out soon enough. Just don't make trouble or things'll go very badly for you.'

'What sort of trouble can I make like this,' said Ivan, presenting his bound wrists for inspection.

The bald man urged him up a flight of wooden steps to a back verandah. Ivan glanced to his right over the dividing fence to the Sherring's backyard. The old Hills Hoist was still there, but a new swing set had replaced the old rope swing Mr Sherring had strung up from a tree, which also had gone.

'C'mon,' said the bald man, prodding him in the ribs. 'Get a move on.'

The back verandah opened into a kitchen which Ivan judged to be many decades out of style.

From the kitchen Ivan was man-handled into a hall which led to the front door. The first room on the left … in fact all doors opened to the left of the hall … was a small bedroom.

Ivan saw on the wall beside the bedroom door the panel for a burglar alarm.

The bald man warned. 'Yeah. It's a burglar alarm and it's turned on every night when the boss goes to bed so don't even think of trying to get out. The alarm's loud enough to wake the dead and it's got a hair trigger. The neighbours are always complaining.'

The next door opened to a study which featured a modern chrome desk with a word processor on it. The screen displayed neat rows of icons.

Ivan's escort brought him to a halt at the next door. 'This is where we part company for the present,' the bald man said, turning the bow of the old fashioned key in the lock.

The man pushed the door in and reached around to turn on a light.

Ivan saw flight of stairs leading down to a cellar which was dimly lit by a single unshaded bulb hanging from a high ceiling.

'You mean you're putting me down there?' he asked nervously.

'That's the idea,' the man said cheerfully. He took a pocket knife from his slacks pocket and removed the tape binding Ivan's wrists before pushing him towards the top of the stairs.

When he reached the cellar floor Ivan turned. 'And how long do you intend to keep me down here?'

'That's not up to me,' said the bald man. He closed the door firmly and Ivan heard the key turn.

He looked about him. It was a large room. There was a bed with blankets on it, folded neatly at one end. An open door showed a tiled bathroom with a w.c. and an old fashioned shower. Apart from the bed the room was empty except for an ancient wardrobe. One door was sagging open to show a coat rail with a group of wire coat hangers clustered at one end.

The only window was in the wall opposite the stairs and it was so high that Ivan could see only a patch of sky.

He glanced at his watch. It was eleven a.m. He calculated

he had left Mary's flat to go to the shops just after nine. Shopping had taken little more than an hour and the walk home, he knew, was no more than twenty minutes. That left about forty minutes unaccounted for. He knew that the house where they had brought him was near the harbour and would certainly account for most of the forty minutes. So chances were that he had been unconscious for much of those forty minutes since he had regained his senses only as the car arrived at its destination.

Ivan removed his shoes and lay down on the bed, placing one of the folded blankets under his head for a pillow.

Then he turned his mind to escape. Knowing where the house was located was an advantage since he would have good local knowledge assuming things in the neighbourhood had not changed too much in the decades since he lived in the next street.

But local knowledge was of no use until he was out of doors and could put his knowledge to work.

Step one. How to escape from the room. That was a big enough hurdle to leap in itself.

He closed his eyes and began to think.

*   *   *

When Hodgkiss heard the unmarked police car pull up in the driveway around six o'clock he put down the newspaper he had been reading in the wingback chair in the living room and hurried down the hall to the kitchen.

Donald was already in the breakfast nook, a can of beer in his hand.

Before Hodgkiss could get a word out Donald raised a hand. 'Please, Dad. No more. I agreed to see this Ivan fellah although I didn't want to. He didn't show. That's it. I can't do any more. So please, can we just leave it there?'

'Very well, Donald. I'll keep it brief. Crane has disappeared. He went out early this morning and has not returned. So either you begin an investigation into his disappearance now, with a fair chance of finding him in one piece, or you can delay, fob off the inevitable, and before the end of the week start an investigation into his murder. The choice is yours.'

'Well thanks for giving me a choice, Dad. And what makes you think I could find him even if I started looking for him now?'

'I think it would be a relatively simple matter. We know the people responsible for his abduction ....'

'And what makes you so sure he's been abducted?'

'Because I know there has already been one attempt ... the attempt I saw and foiled. And now he's missing so those who failed the first time have no doubt succeeded on their second attempt.'

'And if I did agree to investigate this alleged abduction ... which I don't ... where would I start?'

'With his employers, of course. The people who feared he would destroy their reputation and their business by exposing their chicanery.'

'You seriously expect me to turn up at this place, a reputable pharmaceutical company, and start questioning his boss ... I don't even know the fellow's name.'

'His boss's name is Forrest,' Hodgkiss supplied.

'Well, quizzing this Forrest about one of his employees disappearing because he was scared that Forrest had arranged for criminals to murder him because he'd found out they were faking some test results.'

Hodgkiss nodded. 'I believe that would be an entirely appropriate line of inquiry. Wouldn't you agree?'

'No, I would not agree. It might be an entirely appropriate line of inquiry if I had a shred of evidence that they'd done anything wrong. I don't even have a statement from the person making the allegation. I'd make a complete fool of myself.'

'Well, as I said before, Donald. If you don't act now you will soon be undertaking a murder investigation.'

'But what makes you think this guy Crane is in any danger now.'

'He left the home of his friend Mary Corbett at nine o'clock this morning and has not been seen since. His phone is turned off which I am assured is most unusual. He does not enjoy robust health and I believe there is real cause for alarm.'

Donald shook his head. 'Sorry, Dad. You know I can't just dive in and start an investigation on your say so when there's just nothing solid to go on. He'll probably turn up tonight ... or some time soon.'

'And what about the registration number of that car I gave you. What have you done about that? Nothing, I suppose.'

'I gave that to Sergeant Sanderson to have a look at it.'

'Oh wonderful,' said Hodgkiss. 'You might as well have dropped it straight into the wastepaper basket.'

Hodgkiss pushed angrily out of the breakfast nook and stamped back down the hall to his bedroom at the front of the house, thumbing Esme's borrowed mobile phone as he went.

'I tried, but he wouldn't listen,' he told Mary. 'Ring when you hear anything ... anything at all.'

*　*　*

The light in the high window was failing when Ivan heard the door at the top of the steps unlock. The door swung inwards and the bald man set a tray of food down on the top step. The door was closed again and locked.

Ivan made his way quickly up the steps and set to on the meal which consisted of hamburger mince, chips, a flood of tomato sauce and a polystyrene mug of luke warm instant coffee.

Her made a silent apology to his stomach as he bolted down the food.

He left the tray and the empty dishes where he had found them, but before he returned to the cellar floor he turned off the light and sank to his knees on he second step.

Through a gap at the bottom of the door he could make out a swathe of beige carpet in the brightly lit hall outside.

He nodded thoughtfully as he turned the light back on and retreated carefully down to the cellar floor.

But instead of returning to the bed he made a detour to the wardrobe where he removed one of the wire coat hangers from the rail. He returned to the bed where he applied himself to the task of untwisting the hook of the hanger then straightening the wire, although several kinks remained in its length to mark where it had been bent.

One end of the wire he twisted into a hook.

Then he settled back on the bed, eyes closed, a smile on his face.

He discovered with some surprise that he was looking forward to the coming hours of darkness.

About an hour later Ivan heard the lock turn and the door opened. The bald man stooped and picked up the tray.

Ivan called. 'Would you mind turning off the light if it's not too much trouble. I've had a rather trying day and would like to get some sleep.'

The bald man grunted, the light went out, the door closed and the lock was turned.

Now the only light in the room was from the crack under the door at the top of the stairs and from a gibbous moon that peeped eerily through the window.

Ivan moved the bed so that he could see the light under the door when he lay down. The he settled down to think in detail of what he planned to do later that night.

It was seeing the word processor in the next room that had given him the idea. His only reservation about the scheme was his own lack of skill with those blasted machines.

He had never been properly trained in the use of a word processor and his lack of proficiency was a joke in the office. Often he had to call one or other of the staff, usually one of the young women who were quite obliging, to assist him when he encountered some problem with a programme he was using or even when such elementary things occurred as a hung screen or a disappearing cursor.

But he could perform most of the elementary tasks such as opening a new document, cutting and pasting, saving a document or opening, writing and sending an email.

Ivan fought the temptation to give way to sleep, but in vain. He awoke with a start, panicked to see that the light under the door had gone out. He glanced upwards and was relieved to see that a small arc of the moon was still visible at edge of the window, suggesting that he had not been long asleep.

He walked on tiptoe to the top of the stairs, dropped to his knees and looked through the gap at the bottom of the door. Somewhere a nightlight was giving a faint illumination to the carpet.

Then he applied an ear to the wooden door and listened intently.

Nothing. All was quiet.

'I'll give it another hour,' he thought, and tiptoed back to the bed, glancing at the luminous dial of his watch.

When an hour had passed … fifty-three minutes to be exact … Ivan picked up the wire from the floor beside the bed and returned up the stairs to the door.

Ivan had seen and read several works of fiction where the hero, locked in a room with the key left in the lock on the outside, had escaped by dislodging the key onto a sheet of paper, pulling the paper back under the door and thus freeing himself.

Ivan had noted that there was an adequate gap between the bottom of the door and the hall carpet, but his problem was that there was no paper in the room. Not a single sheet. But, Ivan decided, the wire coat hanger would serve the same purpose. He could use the hook he had made at one end of the wire to manoeuvre the key back under the door.

He inserted the straight end of the wire into the lock and began to wiggle and push.

To his amazement the key fell out almost at once.

He crouched on the second step and looked under the door. By the dim light inf the hall the key was plainly visible resting on the carpet.

It was a simple matter, using the hooked end of the clothes hanger, to draw the key back under the door.

Ivan put the key into the lock and turned it slowly. He pulled the door open and looked cautiously up and down the hall.

He stood still, listening. Somewhere to his left an electric motor cut in … probably a refrigerator, he thought.

The word processor he had seen was in the next room towards the back door.

Ten cautious paces brought him to the door, which was closed.

He turned the handle and pushed the door open a few inches and listened. Nothing. He pushed the door wide, stepped quickly into the room and closed the door behind him.

Ivan took his seat at the computer with misgivings. He searched the screen for the icon that would open the email.

He found the icon, moved the cursor to it and clicked the mouse. At once the screen showed the inbox with its list of emails.

He moved the cursor to the box for New Email and clicked.

The format for a new email appeared.

He moved the cursor to the top window marked 'To …'

This was the tricky bit. He did not know Mary Corbett's private email address, if she had one, but he had assumed that this computer may be linked to the company's network.

In the top window he put in the letter 'm'.

Immediately a small window opened giving the email addresses of a number of people who worked for the company whose names began with an 'm.'

But Mary's email address was not among them.

He deleted the m and inserted a 'c.'

Again several email addresses appeared and among them was corbettm@iinet.com.au

Ivan clicked on it and Mary's email address appeared in the 'To…' window.

He paused for a moment, thinking, then began to type. Because he was not a trained typist Ivan's eyes were on the keyboard as he hunted and pecked his way through the message.

When finally he looked up at the screen he was horrified at what he saw.

He3d 5n r660 at 9 P832 C36se 8802 5van

How on earth had that got there?

But before he had a chance to begin to retype the message the door behind him flew open.

It was the bald man. 'What the hell are you doing there?'

Ivan moved the cursor quickly to the Send key and clicked the mouse.

The message went.

'What have you been doing?' the bald man demanded. 'And how the hell did you get out of the cellar?'

'What's going on here?' It was the dark man, newly wakened and unhappy.

'I think he just sent an email,' said the bald man.

'You think?' the dark man snapped. 'Then we'd better have a look at what he sent.'

The dark man moved the icon to the Sent box and clicked. The Sent column appeared with the email addressed to Mary Corbett at the top.

The dark man clicked on the top email and the text appeared.

He laughed. 'He might be clever at escaping, but I tell you what, he's a dud typist' he said.

He turned to the bald man. 'Put him back down there and make sure he stays there this time. Meanwhile I'd better tell the boss what's happened.'

When the bald man returned Ivan to the cellar he had demanded to know how Ivan had escaped. Ivan had avoided the issue simply by insisting that the door had been left unlocked.

The bald man, not wishing to have this explanation shared with his partner, did not stay to debate the matter.

This time he took the key away with him after locking the door.

*   *   *

Arthur Forrest was not pleased.

He had just been informed that Ivan Crane, the man who had spied on the company's testing programme, no doubt with the intention of causing the company grievous financial harm, had somehow sent an email to one of the female staff … the office receptionist, Mary Corbett.

Ms Corbett, he had just been informed, had not yet reported for work and another member of staff was attending to her duties at the reception desk.

Unfortunately this email appeared to have been sent in some kind of code and he had set the two men in charge of the testing programmes, Ferris and Morris, to work to extract its meaning.

He read the one-line email for umpteenth time.

He3d 5n r660 at 9 P832 C36se 8802 5van

He shook his head, still baffled.

No doubt Crane and the Corbett woman had worked out some secret code to use in their clandestine communications.

Well, when she turns up here, if she turns up here, I'll damn soon find out from her what it means and I won't mind how I do it. The gloves will be off.

Just then Jerry Ferris and Barry Morris knocked and entered.

'Any joy,' Forrest asked without any real hope of receiving an encouraging reply.

Ferris shook his head. 'We're still working on it, Arthur. What about you? Any ideas?'

Forrest shook his head. 'Those four numbers near the end. Could they be a postcode?'

Morris shook his head. 'No postcodes start with 8. I checked the postcode book … nothing.'

Ferris suggested. 'Perhaps one of us should go out and see the girl?'

Forrest shook her head. 'No. Best leave her alone.'

'Office gossip was that she had a bit of a crush on Crane. Do you think it'd be an idea to keep an eye on her? Stake out her place?'

'What on earth for?' Forrest asked.

'Well, she could lead us to him.'

'But we don't need her to lead us to him; we know where he is … that is if that pair of clowns can hold on to him. He got out of the cellar somehow last night and probably would have made a break for it if he hadn't known about the burglar alarm.'

'But don't you think we should know who she talks to … who she sees?'

Forrest thought about that. 'Give it a day or two. See how things work out. See if we can crack this code.'

*   *   *

While this speculation was continuing Mary Corbett was engaged in some speculation of her own.

She was convinced now that somehow the men who had attempted to abduct Ivan before, had made a second attempt and this time they had succeeded.

She was confident that if he *had* been abducted he would surely attempt to contact her, if he was able to do so.

However there was a problem. Or rather two problems. First he did not know her mobile phone number. Secondly he did not know her private email address.

But of course he knew her email address at work and he may attempt to contact her there.

So Mary logged into her computer at work, went to the

inbox of her email and found an email had arrived there shortly after one in the morning.

While it might have been sent from Ivan – in fact the last word of the message was almost his name, 5van — unfortunately none of it made any sense.

She read it through a second time and shook her head.

If she was to work this out she was going to need help. But who could help her?

Perhaps she should forward the email to Mr Hodgkiss and perhaps he could persuade his son-in-law, the detective, to put some of the experts in the police force onto the job. They should crack the code in no time, assuming it was a code and not just really bad typing. But even Ivan would not send a message that had been typed so illegibly.

Somewhere or other she'd made a note of Mr Hodgkiss' phone number. She'd ring him and tell him about the email and if he thought he could help she could forward it to him.

'It's someone called Mary,' said Esme, handing her mobile phone to Hodgkiss. She added: 'I do wish you'd buy yourself another phone instead of using mine all the time. How many other people have you given my number to?'

Hodgkiss ignored the rebuke. 'Yes, Mary. Have you heard from Ivan? Is he back?'

'No. He's not back. And I know this sounds strange, but I don't know if I've actually heard from him or not.'

'"You don't know if you've heard from him". How is that possible?'

'Well, someone, it could have been Ivan, sent an email to my office computer, but the trouble is it makes no sense.'

'In what way?'

'It's weird. It looks like it's in some kind of code. Everything's all jumbled up. There's hardly a proper word in the whole message.'

'Well, what does it say?'

'If you'll give me your email address I'll forward it to you and you see what you can make of it.'

Five minutes later Hodgkiss had the message on the screen of his computer.

At the same time Esme's phone, now in Hodgkiss shirt pocket, rang again. Mary asked. 'Have you got it?'

'Yes. I'm looking at it now,' said Hodgkiss, 'and I regret to say that a solution does not spring immediately to mind. As you say, it could be a code of some kind. If so it might take some time to crack.'

'But I don't think Ivan knew anything about codes. Besides, we mightn't have much time,' said Mary, near to tears. 'Heaven knows what they'll do to him, particularly if they've found out that he's sent me a message. What about your son-in-law. Do they have experts in codes and that sort of thing in the police force?'

'Very likely,' said Hodgkiss. 'But the problem will be persuading Donald to take an intelligent interest in the matter.'

'But he knows about those men trying to kidnap Ivan, doesn't he?'

'Yes, he knows about that, although I doubt if he was convinced that it was really an attempted kidnapping.'

'Did he know about that man Voce and his reputation?'

Yes, he knew about that too, but I fear we're going to need more than that if Donald is to be any use to us.'

'But I don't see what else we can do.'

'Nor do I, at the moment. Leave it with me, Mary. I'll try him again and get back to you.'

He printed the email from the screen and took it with him

to the kitchen where Donald was wedged into the break-fast nook finishing a huge meal of bacon, eggs, tomato and mushrooms.

Hodgkiss slid into the narrow bench seat opposite and set down the email, turned to face towards Donald.

A fork laden with fried egg and tomato was half way to Donald's mouth when he saw the paper. The fork's journey was arrested briefly when Donald's glance fell on the paper. There was a shake of the head and the fork continued on its journey.

As Esme set down a mug of black tea in front of Donald she, too, saw the paper.

'And what's that bit of nonsense all about, Dad?' she asked unsympathetically.

'That,' said Hodgkiss dramatically, 'is a desperate message from an unfortunate man who even now may be facing an awful death.'

'Well, he should have learned to spell,' said Esme, removing the empty plate from in front of Donald. 'He's got no chance if he can't spell well enough to tell people where he is or even put his name on it.'

'But his name is on it,' said Hodgkiss, 'and the location where he is being held.'

'Good. Problem solved then,' said Donald, dabbing his lips with a paper serviette. 'You won't need me to help.'

'No, Donald, I don't need *you* to help. To seek help from you is a futile endeavour at any time.'

'Then good luck,' said Donald, finishing his mug of tea in two mighty swallows, 'because I've got proper police work to do. I've got no time to waste on silly games like that.'

Hodgkiss snatched up the paper and stamped back down the hall to his room.

Esme came to the hall door and called after him: 'And if you don't do something to tidy your room I'll come down there and do it for you. It must be months since you've dusted.'

Hodgkiss stopped and turned angrily. 'You will kindly leave my room exactly as it is. I don't want you interfrering with my things. Last time you tidied up I couldn't find anything for months.'

But later in the morning, when Hodgkiss had returned from a late walk with Rupert, he was in time to see Esme exiting his bedroom pushing the vacuum cleaner and with a dusting cloth in the other hand.

'There you are, Dad,' she said. 'All done and I put everything back exactly where I found it. With all that dust lying around it's a wonder you weren't sneezing your head off.'

Hodgkiss walked past her without a word, entered the bedroom and closed the door heavily behind him.

He pulled back the captain's chair in front of his desk and settled in front of the computer. He checked his emails to see if there was a further message from Mary.

When there was none he decided to forward Mary's email with the cryptic line to Pat Strong with an appeal for help.

He clicked on the forward box and when the new message appeared he moved the cursor to the 'To...' box, typed in the letter 's' and, as usual, Pat's full email address appeared.

strongp@iinet.com.au

Hodgkiss moved the cursor down and began typing.

Dear Pat,

The 35ne be36w was rece5vfed th5s 06rn5ng fr60

Hodgkiss stopped typing. He stared at the screen, baffled. He pushed the send button then took the phone from his pocket and pecked at the keypad.

'Pat. I've just sent you an email. Will you look at it and tell me what ... if anything ... you can make of it. I'll wait on.'

In the study of her town house in nearby Kylerbrin, Pat Strong glanced at her computer screen.

'I'm on the computer now,' she said, 'and your email's just arrived. Hold on a moment, Hodgkiss.'

Pat opened her email and clicked on the latest message.

'Your typing isn't improving Hodgkiss' she said.

'Never mind my typing,' Hodgkiss snapped testily. 'What about the other line ... the message in the attachment I forwarded ... one ending "5van"?'

'Yes, I see it. What about it?'

'What do you mean "What about it?" It's not just bad typing is it? It's something else, isn't it? There must be something wrong.'

'Of course there's something wrong and only a technological Neanderthal like you would have failed to recognise it.'

'All right, Mrs Einstein, what have I failed to recognise?'

'Have you got a pencil and paper handy. I'll tell you what's happened.'

*　*　*

Donald was not pleased. 'How many times have I told you never to ring on this number.'

Hodgkiss was ready. 'You have never told me that. You have told me on several occasions never to ring on this number *except in the case of a dire emergency.* I have a situation that amply meets that criterion.'

'What are you talking about, Dad? What situation ... what criterion?'

'Donald. Listen carefully; I know where Ivan Crane's kidnappers are holding him. It is some distance away. To delay for even a moment is to play Russian roulette with the man's life … if we are not already too late.'

'Are you telling me that you worked out an address from that jumble of letters and numbers?'

'No, Donald. I didn't work it out. Pat did.'

'How did Pat …?'

'Donald, we are wasting time. I will explain it on the way. Can you come now and collect me?'

'No, Dad, I can not come now and collect you. Believe it or not I have actual police work to do … and plenty of it at the moment. So if you would care to wait …'

But Hodgkiss did not care to wait. He cut the connection and immediately redialed the number for Mary Corbett.

'Mary, I have the address where they are holding Ivan. I have spoken to my son-in-law and he has flatly refused to assist. In view of that I believe we have no alternative but to go there ourselves and deal with these people as best we can. Are you prepared to do that?'

'Of course I am, Edgar. Do you want me to pick you up? How far is it … this place where you think they're holding Ivan?'

'It is some distance. Do you have a street directory?'

'I have a GPS. I'm on my way.'

Hodgkiss closed his computer, scribbled the address *9 Polk Close* on a piece of paper and hurried down the hall to the kitchen.

'Esme, a young lady will be calling for me shortly. We will be going to this address,' he said placing the paper on the kitchen bench. 'I have just spoken to Donald and appealed to him to assist me in this matter and he has refused.'

Esme asked anxiously. 'Is this about the fellow who was supposed to have been kidnapped?'

'There is no "supposed to have been" about it, Esme. The fellow is being held prisoner at that address. I will be going there now with Ms Corbett to release him.'

'Dad, have you taken leave of your senses!? If the people there have really kidnapped this fellow how do you think you're going to make them let him go? They'll probably kidnap you too.'

'Esme, someone has to do something to help the poor man … if it is not already too late.'

'Don't you dare go, Dad. I forbid it. I know how crazy and headstrong you can be when it comes to this sort of thing.'

'You think, do you, that I should just stand by and wait for Donald to come to his senses and recognise that the matter is urgent. I'm sorry, Esme, I don't have time for that. If you like you can contact him when I've gone and see if you can persuade him that the matter is urgent and give him that address.'

Hodgkiss went out through the laundry then down the driveway just as Mary Corbett's small sedan stopped at the kerb.

For the next three quarters of an hour Hodgkiss and Mary sat in near silence waiting for the next electronic prompt, given in prim female tones, to guide them to their destination.

At last came the final snippet of instruction: 'Approaching your destination one hundred metres on the left.'

'Don't stop,' said Hodgkiss. 'Drive past and I'll have a look at the place.'

Nine Polk Close was a rather dilapidated brick bungalow with a driveway on one side and a car port at the rear.

Hodgkiss noted that a large dark sedan, similar to the one used in the attempted abduction of Ivan Crane, was parked in the car port.

'It's the place all right,' he said. 'That car I saw before is parked at the rear. Stop here.'

Mary parked the car and pulled on the handbrake. 'What now?' she asked nervously.

'Well, we haven't come all this way to sit in the car, have we,' said Hodgkiss. 'I suggest you stay here and I'll go and let them know that their little game is over and that it will go easier for them if they release Ivan now, unharmed.'

'And what will you do if they refuse?'

'How can they refuse? The very fact that I'm there on their doorstep will be proof that their whereabouts is known and I'll tell them that the police are on their way.'

'They might think you're bluffing,' Mary suggested.

'Why would they think that?'

'Because you would be bluffing, wouldn't you?'

'Yes, perhaps, but they wouldn't know that.'

Mary shook her head. 'I don't like it. If you're going in I'm coming with you.'

Hodgkiss shrugged. 'Very well. Then let's not sit around talking about.'

He pushed open the passenger's door and climbed out on the footpath where Mary joined him.

*   *   *

Esme was looking out of the kitchen window at the back garden, but she was seeing nothing.

Her mind was in turmoil.

She knew there were decisions, important decisions to be made and very little time in which to make them.

Her father and some woman she did not know had just

driven away somewhere … she knew where exactly because he had written the address on a scrap of paper and left it right there on the bench.

She knew that wherever it was the two of them were going they were very likely headed for serious trouble.

She did not know what form the trouble would take but she knew that somewhere in the muddled picture there was that fellow who her father said had been the victim of an attempted kidnapping.

So unwholesome people, would-be kidnappers, were involved somewhere along the line.

She was now confronted with the alternatives, neither of which appealed to her: either she must ring Donald at once and persuade him to travel to that address and sort out whatever situation her father was involved in, or, more likely, had created; or she must go there herself and do the best she could in the circumstances.

She decided to do both.

Since her father had her mobile phone Esme used the landline phone in the hall.

When she rang Donald's number at the Crestwood Police Station the call was diverted to Donald's office and answered by Sergeant Sanderson.

'He's in conference with Superintendent O'Hare' said the sergeant, 'and he left word that he wasn't to be disturbed in any circumstances.'

'But these aren't just any circumstances,' said Esme, 'this is an emergency.'

'I could give him a message when he comes back,' the sergeant offered. 'I'll tell him that it was an emergency.'

'Very well,' said Esme, determined not to waste any more time. 'Tell him his wife rang and that I've gone to number 9

Polk Close. Tell him my father's on his way there now with a young woman because he thinks that's where the kidnappers are holding the man Dad told him about. He'll understand … probably. Now, have you got that?'

'I think so,' said the sergeant. 'But if kidnappers are involved don't you thing you should leave it to the police.'

Esme snapped. 'Of course I should leave it to the police, but the police aren't interested. Dad told Donald all about it but he didn't take a scrap of notice, so now I've got to take care of it myself. Goodness knows what sort of danger my father has got himself into this time and all Donald can do is chat to Mr O'Hare.'

Esme hung up the phone, checked that the piece of paper with the address Hodgkiss had written down, was in her handbag then hurried out to the garage.

Having checked the location of Polk Place in her street directory, Esme set out, feeling confident of reaching her destination without making too many detours.

About the same time that Esme was driving her small beige sedan cautiously along the driveway from the garage to the street, Hodgkiss and Mary Corbett were standing on the nature strip outside 9 Polk Place.

'Well, what do we do now?' Mary asked. 'And what if your friend was wrong and this isn't the place at all.'

'I don't think there's much doubt about the address. It was a very neat solution,' said Hodgkiss. 'But there's only one way to find out. Now, I want you to go back to the car and wait. If I'm not back in ten minutes go for the police.'

'But what will I tell them. Your son-in-law didn't seem to believe what you told him. Why would they believe me?'

Hodgkiss shrugged. 'Well, just do your best,' he said heading for the front gate.

Mary watched anxiously as Hodgkiss walked down the weed-infested path and mounted three rickety wooden steps to the front verandah. He knocked heavily on a brass knocker hanging precariously from the front door.

As soon as the door opened Hodgkiss recognised at once the bald man, one of the two who had attempted to drag Ivan Crane to their car.

And after a moment's hesitation the bald man recognised Hodgkiss.

'What the hell are you doing here?' the bald man demanded.

'You know why I'm here,' said Hodgkiss. 'I've come to collect my friend, Mr Crane.'

'I dunno any Mr Crane,' said the bald man.

'Please, there is no point in playing games with me. The police have been informed. You can release Mr Crane to me now or you can wait until the police arrive and I have no doubt they'll take you and your friend into custody. Kidnapping is a crime that carries a long term of imprisonment.'

'Who's there?' came a voice from behind the bald man.

The bald man turned. 'It's the old guy with the beard who interfered when we tried to grab Crane the first time.'

'Well, where's your manners; invite him in,' said the voice.

The bald man stepped aside and Hodgkiss saw the dark man standing in the doorway of a bedroom to the left.

'Come on in,' said the dark-haired man.

The bald man reached out and took hold of Hodgkiss by the arm and dragged him across the threshold, closing the door firmly behind him.

'There is no need for violence,' Hodgkiss said to the dark man. 'I've come here to take Mr Crane home. You would be wise to release him to me now before the police arrive. I think I might have mentioned on an earlier occasion that my son-in-law is a detective and he is aware of my movements, so it is only a matter of time before he arrives and starts to ask you two some awkward questions.'

'We'll cross those bridges when we come to them,' said the dark man. 'Meanwhile, I suppose you'd like to see your friend Crane, would you?' He turned to the bald man. 'Put him down in the cellar. They can keep each other company until I find out what the boss wants us to do with them.'

The bald man frog-marched Hodgkiss down the hall to the third door where he stopped. took out a key and unlocked then opened the door. 'Down there,' he said, pointing.

Hodgkiss looked down into the cellar. By the light of a single bulb he saw Crane lying on a bed on the far side of the room, his head propped on a pillow of blankets, apparently sleeping.

Then he heard the door behind him slam shut and the lock turn.

This wakened Crane. He sat up. 'Mr Hodgkiss. Thank heavens. It's great to see you. Then someone worked out my message.'

Hodgkiss nodded. 'Yes, it was elementary.'

'But what about Mary. Is she all right?'

'Yes. She's fine. She's outside. I told her to wait in the car.'

For the moment Crane had not grasped the situation. 'But why is she waiting outside? Why didn't she come in?'

Then: 'D'you mean … they've caught you too … that you're a prisoner here too?'

Hodgkiss nodded gloomily.

'But if Mary's outside they might see her and capture her.'

Hodgkiss shook his head confidently. 'No. She'll be on the lookout for them. I warned her to go for the police if I'm not out in ten minutes.'

'Well that should give them something to think about. Surely they'll realise the game's up now. They'll have to let us go.'

Hodgkiss glanced at his watch. 'Ten minutes must be nearly up by now.'

*　　*　　*

Sergeant Sanderson was feeling distinctly uneasy.

Mrs Burke had said the situation … whatever it was … was an emergency.

And now Inspector Burke and the superintendent had finished their conference and gone out somewhere.

Sergeant Sanderson checked on the address Mrs Burke had given … 9 Polk Place… then he rang the police station nearest to the address with a request that they pay an urgent visit to the address, ask if Mrs Burke was there and satisfy themselves that all was well.

Ten minutes later a police patrol car driven by Sergeant Frame with Constable Burton beside him, turned into Polk Place.

'Number nine, wasn't it?' the sergeant asked.

Constable Burton said. 'Yeah, That'll be where the little blue car's parked.

A woman was sitting in the blue car. She scrambled out as soon as the police car parked behind her and came running to the driver's window: 'Oh officer, thank heaven you've come. He said to go for the police if he wasn't out in ten minutes.'

During his twenty-five years in the police force Sergeant Frame had acquired considerable experience in dealing with hysterical women, and this one, a pretty little thing, was up there with the worst of them.

He opened the driver's door and unwound his long frame from behind the wheel. 'One thing at a time, madam,' he said. 'Someone told you to ring the police … is that so?'

'Yes, Mr Hodgkiss. He went in there,' she said, jabbing a frantic finger n the direction of number nine. 'He said to send for the police if he wasn't out in ten minutes. That was nearly twenty minutes ago. I was just about to ring.'

'So this Mr Hodgkiss … he went in to number nine and he thought perhaps he might not be able to come out again. Is that what you're saying?'

'Yes, you see that was because …'

Sgt Frame stopped her in mid-flow. 'One thing at a time please Miss ….'

'Corbett … Mary Corbett.'

'So why did he think he might not be able to come out again?'

'Because that's where the kidnappers are … in there.'

'The kidnappers? And how do you know there are kidnappers in there?'

'Because that's where they're holding my friend Ivan Crane. He sent me a message … an email.'

'He sent an email saying he's being held captive at this address. Is that correct?'

'Yes, of course. Now can we please go in and get him … and Mr Hodgkiss.'

'You say your friend Mr Crane sent you an email giving this address.'

'Yes, that's right.'

'May I see it please?'

'Just a moment,' said Mary. She dipped into a deep shoulder bag and came out with her mobile phone. She turned it on and began scrolling through her messages.

'Here you are,' she said, handing the phone to the sergeant. 'It's a bit jumbled, but they worked out that this is the right address.'

Sergeant Frame stared at the screen. No way could he make Polk Place out of the illegible line of numbers and letters on the tiny screen, although there was certainly a 9 there.

He shook his head, bewildered. He turned to Mary and said slowly and with emphasis. 'I am not about to knock on that door and begin asking questions on the basis of *that*,' he said, holding the screen towards Mary.

'But Mr Hodgkiss worked it out … the address. I don't know how, but he was sure it said Polk Place.'

'And this Mr Hodgkiss is the fellow who went inside, right?'

'Yes, and he's still in there. Please can we just go to the door and ask for him and for Ivan Crane? If you won't I will.'

When Sergeant Frame showed no sign of agreeing Mary turned and headed for the front gate.

Half way up the front path she paused, then stepped sideways onto the lawn and, walking quickly, disappeared around the corner of the house.

Sergeant Frame climbed back into his patrol car. 'We'll give her five minutes, radio in that there was nothing here then we'd better go back to the station.'

But they did not have to wait five minutes.

In less than two minutes they saw Mary running across the lawn towards the front path.

She arrived at the police car breathless.

'They're both in a cellar. There's a little window near the ground at the side of the house. I saw them … both of them. They told me they can't get out. Now will you please come?'

The two officers glanced at each other sceptically, but climbed out.

'Now, where's this window,' Sergeant Frame asked.

Minutes later Sergeant Frame was on his hands and knees in a garden bed looking down through a small window, almost at ground level.

Both of the occupants of the cellar, an elderly man with a short grey beard and a second man, of slight build and aged about forty, confirmed that they were being held prisoner and that they wished to be released.

The two policemen, with Mary hard on their heels, walked around to the front door where Sergeant Frame wielded the knocker with vigour.

But almost at once they heard the sound of a motor starting somewhere at the rear of the house then moments later a dark sedan sped down the driveway on the other side of the property, swung into the street with tyres squealing, and drove away at high speed.

The sergeant with the constable and Mary in his wake walked quickly around the house and climbed to the back verandah where the kitchen door was standing open.

Mary pushed past the two officers and ran down the hall towards the front of the house. She stopped at one of the doors on the right of the hall.

'Ivan, are you in there,' she called. 'And you, Mr Hodgkiss.'

Sergeant Frame could make out muffled replies.

Just then someone started to beat energetically with the knocker on the front door.

Sergeant Frame turned to his constable. 'See what the hell that's about, will you, constable, and I'll see what I can do about getting these people out.'

Constable Burton pulled back the front door to see a rather attractive middle-aged woman with curly blonde hair standing on the doormat. She looked both alarmed and angry.

She said. 'My name's Esme Burke and my father is being held prisoner in there somewhere.'

Constable Burton noticed a small beige sedan was parked behind the patrol car.

* * *

'We picked up Ken Voce and his buddy Baldy Roberts on the Northern Highway just the other side of Hornby. Baldy' s singing like a canary.'

Inspector Donald Burke made this welcome announcement to those gathered around the redwood table on the back deck of his Lillimoor home.

On the table was a bottle of white wine, now nearly empty, and a scattering of wine glasses and biscuit crumbs.

Esme turned to Hodgkiss, seated beside her. 'And let it be a lesson to you, Dad, not to go running off on some little frolic on your own. See what trouble you can get into and how much trouble you can make for others. You had half the New South Wales police force out looking for you.'

Hodgkiss defended stoutly. 'Really, Esme, that is a gross exaggeration. And besides, I would have had no need to take matters into my own hands if Donald had shown sufficient commonsense and nous to realise that what I'd been telling him was ...'

'And that's enough of that too, Dad,' Esme snapped. 'Do you really think that Donald's got nothing better to do with his time than to run after you when you take it into your head to do something silly.'

Hodgkiss exploded. '"Something silly". Well, if I hadn't done something silly, as you call it, Mr Crane here would be still rotting in that cellar ... or worse.'

Ivan Crane, who was seated cosily beside Mary Corbett, nodded. 'Yes, and I wouldn't have finished up locked in that damned cellar if I hadn't gone downstairs at work that day to use my puffer and if those two fellows, Ferris and Morris, hadn't seen me.'

'Yeah, well you won't have to bother about them for a while,' said Donald. 'They're down at the station now assisting police with their inquires, as they say. And we've got some of the people from our fraud squad at your office as we speak, going through the records of all the testing programmes they've run over the past five years. From results so far it looks like this latest rort wasn't the first test those two have fiddled.'

'And what about Arthur Forrest?' Mary asked. 'From what I've been told it was Forrest who arranged to have those thugs kidnap Ivan.'

Donald nodded. 'Yes, that's what Baldy Roberts told us. But of course it's just his word against Forrest and Baldy isn't known for his honesty. And of course Voce isn't saying anything. He's a professional and we won't get anything much out of him.'

'And another thing,' said Donald, 'after the way Dad's always run Sergeant Sanderson down in the past I think it's worth mentioning that if it hadn't been for Sanderson showing a bit of initiative and contacting the local police and asking them to go and have a look-see at that address, well, the two of them might never have been rescued in time.'

'Yes, that's right, Dad,' said Esme. 'You're always running Sergeant Sanderson down at every opportunity so I reckon you owe him an apology.'

But before Hodgkiss could comment they heard the sound of a car door slamming in the driveway at the side of the house.

Hodgkiss got up. 'That'll be Pat now.'

'And about time too,' said Esme. 'I won't be able to sleep tonight until I know how she worked out the address of that place from the jumble of letters and numbers Ivan put in his email to Mary.'

'Well, you'll sleep sound enough, Esme,' said Hodgkiss, 'because here's Pat to answer all your questions.'

Hodgkiss greeted Pat with a kiss at the top of the steps up from the driveway to deck.

'I hope you've saved some wine for Pat,' he added.

'That's all right,' said Pat, producing a bottle from a leather carry bag. 'I've brought one of my own just in case. I know just how hopelessly disorganized Hodgkiss can be.'

'Not *that* hopelessly disorganized,' said Hodgkiss. 'Not so disorganized that I couldn't play my part in the arrest of two dangerous thugs and the exposure of a group of despicable white-collar criminals who thought nothing of putting the public's health and welfare at risk.'

Donald was determined that his father-in-law should not enjoy any limelight to which he was not entitled.

'Oh come off it, Dad,' he said. 'If it hadn't been for Sergeant Sanderson you'd still be locked up in that cellar.' Then before Hodgkiss could join battle Donald turned quickly to Pat. 'Come on Pat, tell us; how on earth did you do it? How did you work out the right address from that crazy email?'

Pat took a sip of wine. 'There's no big mystery. Whoever sent the email ...'

'That was me,' said Ivan. 'I'm the first to admit I'm not much of a typist. Whenever I type I have to look down at the keyboard to find the right letters. When I finished typing that email and I looked up at the screen ... well, I just couldn't believe my eyes. I didn't have a clue what had happened, what

I'd done wrong … and I still don't. And I didn't have time to try to write it all again because that bald man walked in and saw me. So I just sent it as it was hoping that someone would be able to sort it out.'

'And luckily someone was,' said Esme, 'but I still don't know how. Come on, Pat. For heaven's sake tell us before I scream.'

'As I said a moment ago, there's no big mystery about it. When Ivan typed the email he had the number lock on.'

'And what on earth is the number lock?' Esme asked.

'It's an arrangement you'll find on most word processors,' said Pat. 'It works like this: when the number lock is turned on some of the letter keys, not all of them, only a few, come up on the screen as numbers.'

For a moment Hodgkiss was lost for words. 'But why would they make an arrangement like that? Just to confuse people?'

Pat conceded. 'I must admit I've always regarded it as a rather pointless innovation. I've never used it myself.'

'But how did it happen,' Hodgkiss asked. 'I'm sure I never turned it on before I forwarded Mary's email to you. Not knowingly.'

'But you could have turned it on without realising it. You only have to touch the right key.'

Then he remembered. 'Of course, Esme was in here this morning tidying my room,' he turned to glare at his daughter … 'and dusting.'

'There you are then,' said Pat. 'If she dusted your keyboard vigourously enough she could have turned the number lock on.'

'Of course I dusted your silly computer, Dad. It was thick with dust and I don't know how you ever saw anything on the screen. It was filthy.'

'We can discuss this later, Esme, 'said Hodgkiss. 'Now, Pat, how do I turn the damned things off?'

'Simple. You just press the same key again. You'll probably find it somewhere up towards the right hand top corner of the key board. It probably has Num Lk on it or something like that. Just press it once and you should be back in business. It operates on only a few of the letters and most of them are up in the same part of the keyboard. If you'd known about it you would have had no trouble working out what Ivan's message meant.'

Pat reached into her handbag and took out a scrap of paper. She unfolded it and put it down on the table.

'When I received Mary's email I turned on the number lock on my computer and began to experiment to see which letter keys were part of the programme and what numbers came up when I pressed them.'

She pointed to the scrap of paper. 'Here's what I found –
u=4 i=5 o=6 j=1 k=2 l=3 and m=0.

'Once I knew which numbers matched which letters it was a simple matter to work out what the email said –

Held in room at 9 Polk Close 8802 Ivan.

Pat continued. 'Hodgkiss assumed that the four numbers near the end of the sentence were an inverted post code which he confirmed by finding Polk Close listed with a 2088 code.'

Esme shook her head. 'That was really clever or you, Pat. I don't know what would have happened to those two if you hadn't worked it out as quickly as you did.'

'Nonsense,' said Pat. 'Anyone who knew anything about how word processors work would have tumbled to it in no time.'

'Maybe you're right,' said Mary, 'but time was something we didn't have. I don't know what those ghastly men would have done to Ivan and Mr Hodgkiss if we hadn't arrived when we did.'

Donald said: 'I can tell you what would have happened to them. According to Baldy, and there's no reason to doubt him, Forrest told Voce that he wanted both of them to disappear and never be heard of again. No doubt Voce had interpreted that in the obvious way; they were to be quietly disposed of. Naturally Forrest denies saying anything of the sort and Voce is saying absolutely nothing.'

'Well, Hodgkiss,' said Pat, 'I think it's true to say there's a lesson for you in this, wouldn't you agree?'

'No doubt,' Hodgkiss conceded. 'But I think all of us could learn something from it; Donald should learn to take heed when I warn him that some crime has been or is about to be committed; Mary and Ivan should brush up their word processing skills and Esme should not go vacuuming and dusting in rooms where she has been asked to stay away.'

The uproar that greeted this assessment seemed to amuse Hodgkiss rather than chasten him.

www.ingramcontent.com/pod-product-compliance
Lightning Source LLC
Chambersburg PA
CBHW030428120726
47903CB00003B/859